The Piper Anderson Series

Book 1: Chasing Justice

Book 2: Cutting Ties

Book 3: Changing Fate

Sign up for the mailing list at AuthorDanielleStewart.com
to be notified as soon as a new book comes out.

Cutting Ties

Book 2 of the
Piper Anderson Series

By Danielle Stewart
Copyright © 2013 Danielle Stewart

Print cover by Calista Taylor

Author Contact
Website: AuthorDanielleStewart.com
Email: AuthorDanielleStewart@gmail.com
Facebook: Author Danielle Stewart
Twitter: @DStewartAuthor

Dedication:

To my husband Dave for not just telling me he believes in me, but showing me every day.

Becky, I hit the friend lottery when I found you. Thank you for all you do.

Ruthie, I'm constantly amazed by your selflessness and talent. I hope to make you proud.

My sisters, like everything else in our lives, we do this together.

Bobby

WHEN I BECAME a police officer I swore an oath. "On my honor, I, Robert Murphy Wright, will never betray my badge, my integrity, my character, or the public trust. I will always have the courage to hold myself and others accountable for our actions. I will uphold the constitution, my community, and the agency I serve. So help me God." As I run that last phrase through my mind, I realize it has morphed from an affirmation to a plea. *Help me, God.*

I pledged to tell the truth, to execute the law, because the law is the only thing that separates us from living in a state of anarchy. We are not meant to be judge, jury, and executioner. Falling in love was not supposed to challenge that. They were mutually exclusive ideas. You should be able to love someone and honor your responsibilities at the same time. That is, unless the person you love has been failed by the system so many times she can't trust it. If I'm constantly searching for ways to stand behind the words I swore that day, and she is forever looking for channels that undermine them—can we truly find happiness together?

Meeting Piper, the daughter of a serial murderer, was like winning the worst kind of lottery. No matter how much I try to rationalize it, try to convince myself loving her is dangerous, I can't stop. I watch her battle herself, wondering if the wickedest parts of him are somehow a part of her. She rubs her hand over that scar he left on her leg, the number twenty-three carved so precisely, and I know she fractures a little more. Something broke me the same way it broke her, we just pieced ourselves back together differently.

Witness protection was supposed to be the answer for her.

Edenville was supposed to be her fresh start. Watching her accept the unreserved affection of my friends, Betty and Jules, gave me a hope that maybe she could find peace. Maybe we could find a way to love each other.

But I didn't plan for the fact that her past wasn't quite as buried as she hoped. When I got the call that a girl on campus had been attacked, the number twenty-three carved into her leg, I knew the trajectory of our lives was about to shift. But something doesn't fit. Too many facts don't align with the normal methods of her father, the Railway Killer. Has he found her or is someone emulating his evil? Why use the same number again? Especially considering Piper was not his last victim. Her mother was number twenty-two, and the unfortunate girl killed after Piper's attack was twenty-four. This discrepancy is the small glimmer of hope I'm clinging to.

Yes, I fell in love with a fragmented and damaged girl, but she isn't the only one with a dark past. I have my own secrets, my own history. I begged and fought to know hers with no intention of ever revealing my own. Not to her, not to anyone. With every second that ticks by, every inch closer we get to her past, I'm afraid we'll end up unearthing my own. Life isn't supposed to be this hard, love isn't meant to be this complicated. So why don't I walk away? Those eyes. Those big, brown, old-soul eyes of hers just keep calling out to me. One run of my fingers through her silky, dark hair, one brush of my lips on her skin, and I get dangerously distracted from what I believe.

Chapter One

"I HEARD IT was a crazy scene over at the university. Did you get a peek at that girl's leg? Creepy," Officer Lindsey LaVoie said as she squatted down next to Bobby and laced her boots. He still hadn't gotten used to seeing her in the precinct locker room. It was pretty clear none of the male officers had. Prior to her being allowed in there, many of them had often strutted around naked with their chests puffed out proudly. Now they scurried from the shower to the stalls wrapped in robes or towels. Bobby actually appreciated the change. As far as he was concerned no one should have to look at that many hairy asses before breakfast.

It had been a long battle, Lindsey against the whole department, but she'd finally won. All it took was threats of legal action. Bobby could understand. She just wanted to be treated as an equal, like anyone else on the force. But that was still a far cry from reality. She'd been granted the right to ready herself in the locker room, but her peers found other ways of punishing her for not being a man. They responded just a little slower than normal when she radioed for back up. Partner assignments were like a revolving door after each officer inevitably complained to the captain. Bobby knew when it was his turn to partner with her he'd make it work. Lindsey was as effective as any of the officers he'd worked with, and he trusted she always had his back. They'd formed a casual friendship primarily built on the fact that he didn't treat her like garbage— a low standard but a welcomed change for her.

He watched as she pulled her blond hair into a tight bun with quick precision. It was a good representation of her overall performance on the force. She was incredibly efficient, quick,

3

and reliable. Bobby thought she had a nice face, but her body was built stronger than he preferred. She had a sturdy frame that she worked tirelessly to keep solid and competitive. He had made a point to refrain from deciding if she was attractive or not. To him she was a colleague, and just like Bill Thomly with the buckteeth or Micah Chilling with the handlebar mustache, the way she looked didn't determine how she did her job. The problem was part of him kept wishing he were attracted to her. Wouldn't it be easier to love someone like Lindsey? Knowing that you both believed in doing things the right way, knowing you'd both sworn the same oath. He didn't want to stop loving Piper, his feelings for her were stronger than anything he'd ever felt. The spark when he touched her and the chemistry and bond between them was something he'd waited for his whole life. But as he watched Lindsey he let the stray corners of his mind admit that loving her would be easier, and probably much smarter.

"I didn't see the cut on her leg, but I heard the girl was a wreck," Bobby replied, fighting off his inner voice and reminding himself it was Piper he'd been thinking about all day. She was the one he was counting the minutes until he could hold.

"What do you think? An angry ex-boyfriend or something? It seems kind of sadistic." It wasn't uncommon for Lindsey and Bobby to chat about a crime that had occurred, to brainstorm, but this was different. He did have an idea who it was and why it happened, but he couldn't bring himself to say it.

It had been a long shift, and as late afternoon set in he was ready to get out of there. "I've got to head out. If you hear anything will you give my cell a call? I'd like to stay up to date on it." Bobby slapped her on the shoulder like he would any other officer, but he awkwardly pulled his hand away slowly. Nope, that didn't feel right. Was that too hard, he wondered? Did I make her feel uncomfortable? She read his face and laughed.

"Come on, Bobby, I'm not made of porcelain. Get over yourself." She punched his shoulder and he stumbled back with the force. No, he thought, she was certainly not fragile. "I'll call you if I hear anything," she chuckled. "Have a good one."

Piper hadn't slept in far too long. After hearing about the campus attack that was eerily similar to the attacks her father had committed, Bobby had insisted Piper, Betty, and Jules spend the day at Michael's house. She wanted to say they didn't need a babysitter, but having Michael around did put her mind at ease. They'd be safer there, and though she had faced plenty of danger in her life, this felt different. Piper kept fighting the gnawing feeling that once again she'd roped innocent people into her mess of a life. Betty and Jules had welcomed Piper into their lives so willingly, and all she'd done so far was muddy it up. Michael, the lawyer she suckered into helping take down Judge Lions, kept getting pulled further into her wake of troubles. At some point she expected them all to realize loving her was more trouble than it was worth, and that scared her.

Piper spent the day counting the minutes until Bobby's shift would be over and he could tell her what he'd found out about the campus assault. Did they know who did it? Was it her father? She had wanted to fight sleep and stare out the window until she saw him pulling up, but her eyes grew heavy as lead, her head too weary to hold up. She finally took Michael up on his offer to crash in his bed. It took only a minute before she fell into a fitful sleep.

She'd been haunted by nightmares most of her life, but since she'd moved to Edenville, they'd subsided. With the possibility of her father finding her, that dry spell seemed to be over. Her mind clouded over with a familiar scene. This was a nightmare she'd had before. It wasn't soft around the edges like a dream sequence in a movie. It was sharp, and the way it took her senses hostage made her feel like the prisoner. She couldn't just see the scene, she could smell her father's musk, feel the wobble in her chair. Her sleeping body was helpless now as it overtook her mind.

"This tastes like shit! I swear to God, Coco, you can't cook a meal to save your life. This isn't what I wanted!" her father shouted across their lopsided thrift store kitchen table.

Piper, a smaller version of herself in this dream world, shrank down into her seat. Her father's raised, sharp voice had that effect on her. She was twelve years old. Her father had insisted they sit down for Christmas dinner, something they had never done before. The entire holiday season really meant nothing to her family. There were never presents, special traditions, or family gatherings. The only thing Christmas brought was a more glaring contrast between them and happy families. It was the perfect time of year to realize how little you had.

Her father spoke again, and now he was manic, desperately trying to recreate a scene he'd seen on television. He'd wanted them all to play a part, and so far it wasn't going according to plan. He was spiraling out of control. He'd wanted the house decorated, but her mother couldn't come down from her high long enough to hang the stockings properly. He'd wanted a nice meal, a true holiday dinner, but cooking was something her mother was not capable of. Everything was burnt, or soggy, or cold.

"I told you I wanted this to be like the movie," he hissed, beating his hand on the table. Piper knew what came next. Her father's emotional escalation was the same almost every time he beat them. First he'd bang his fist on a table, a wall, a car. Then he'd throw something. This particular time it was a plateful of freezing-cold instant mashed potatoes. The way they landed with a squishy thud on the floor almost caused Piper to laugh, but she knew it would enrage her father more. Finally, he would toss a few more inanimate objects before moving on to her mother.

It was by no means a one-sided fight. Her mother would defend herself, sometimes even initiate the violence. It was a relationship Piper never understood. *They were two toxic people who brought out the worst in each other, but just couldn't bear to be apart. When one escalated, or spun out of control it seemed to fan the fire in the other.*

There were days Piper could slip away, be forgotten, and escape the wrath. This was not one of those days. Her father's rage was bubbling over as the Christmas scene he had tried to orchestrate fell miles short of his expectation. Now they would pay the price.

Piper shot up in bed, sweating and panting. She heard her own voice whimpering just as she had that day, the Christmas that never was. She looked around the room, trying to get her bearings. Michael's bedroom, she reminded herself. Safe.

She thought back through the dream for a moment, reliving it through the eyes of her younger self, but now processing it as an adult. Piper hadn't known her mother's real name wasn't Coco until she was nineteen years old. She watched her mother fill out a job application and scribble down the name, Caroline Murphy. She often wanted to ask her mother where the nickname came from, how long she had been called Coco, but she never found the right moment. That could sum up much of her relationship with her mother, never quite the right moment to talk, to understand each other, to say the words that sat heavily on their minds.

"You good?" she heard Michael ask, his large frame leaning in the doorway. He had heard her struggling and saw her awaken startled and upset. She drew in a deep, centering breath and nodded her head. Michael was a very calming presence in her life now, and she felt better just seeing him. His sandy blond hair had gotten long in the last few weeks, and he was in need of some gel and a comb. But Michael was one of those men who would have to try really hard not to be attractive. Even as he lost focus on his grooming during this chaotic time, he still looked better than most men who'd put hours of work into their appearance. You couldn't do much to dim the brightness of his emerald eyes or take away from the strength of his boxy, distinguished jaw. He belonged on the cover of a romance novel, his muscular arms lifting the luscious blonde woman with a heaving bosom. His shirt torn open, the skin of his perfectly smooth chest would be a glowing bronze. Yes, Piper thought to herself, if Michael's career as a lawyer was ever to fall apart, he could certainly make some money in other ways.

It took another few minutes after Michael returned to his living room for Piper to gather herself. She smoothed her wild dark hair down and rubbed the rest of the sleep out of her eyes. She glanced over at Michael's sleek alarm clock and realized time had gotten away from her. She leaped from the bed and headed through the apartment toward the window. Without a word, she skipped right by Betty and Jules who were sipping tea around Michael's glass dining room table. Bobby should be here, she thought. He should know what's going on by now. As she peeked out the window, she saw his red pickup pulling in. She ran down the old industrial stairs of Michael's apartment building and burst through the heavy rusted door to greet him.

She felt the knot in her stomach tighten as she read Bobby's grim expression. He stepped out of his truck with heavy shoulders. His dark brown eyes were filled with worry and his jaw was clenched. She couldn't imagine the news would be good, not with that look on his face.

"What did you find out?" she asked, her voice shaking with emotion. The cold air sent a shiver through her. Her thin cotton shirt was no match for the late fall air.

He walked hesitantly toward her, hating to see her sad, wanting to save and warm her all at once. "It's still early in the investigation. The girl is in stable condition. She told detectives she was attacked from behind, and no other witnesses have come forward. It's too soon to know, really. The forensics team is just starting to go over the evidence now. I don't know much more than I did when I left this morning." Bobby opened his arms and she fell wearily into them, letting the muscles of his biceps tighten and curl around her. They were both so tired, physically and emotionally.

She reached up and ran her hand through his short dark hair, and down his neck. It was funny to her that even though they hadn't loved each other long, she seemed to have figured out small yet important things about him. When he was stressed out he stopped shaving, as if the energy to slide the razor down his cheek was too much for him. Or maybe the time spent looking in the mirror made his mind turn over and twist in ways he didn't like. It seemed to change the whole dynamic of his face, but the beginnings of a beard looked good on him. She loved the scratchy sensation it gave against the softness of her palm.

Even in the midst of all this chaos she had to fight the urge to get lost in a passionate moment with him. His touch made this entire thing feel like a distant worry rather than the looming danger it truly was.

"I guess we wait and see what they come up with," Piper murmured, talking into his shoulder as she squeezed him tighter, feeling safe in his arms.

"I think we need to go down to the precinct and tell them what we know. They haven't tied this back to your father at all. No one is even considering the fact that it might be bigger than just some campus crime. It's important they know you're here." Bobby rested his chin on Piper's head and closed his eyes. He knew she wouldn't want to rehash her history, but in his heart he assumed she'd do what was right, even if she did it reluctantly.

"No," she said sharply as she pulled away from him. His chin fell suddenly, sending his teeth into his tongue. It was equally as jarring to Piper. Leaving his arms felt like the shock of a windy day—your hat blowing off your head before you could even raise your arms to try to stop it. She was the one backing up, but it still felt like he was the one being pulled away.

"We have no idea if this is my father or not. Someone could have easily searched the Internet for serial killers and decided they wanted to play lunatic for the day. I'm not going to go shout from the rooftops that I'm here in Edenville only to find out this had nothing to do with me."

Bobby was stunned by her steely tone and met her frustration with his own. "I'm not asking you to go on the ten o'clock news. I'm asking you to come down and talk to the captain. Tell him what you know, who you are. You have a responsibility here."

"Do you think I went on the ten o'clock news back in New York? No. But somehow information was leaked. My father found out I survived and now here I am. If this attack wasn't my father, if it was someone else, I can kiss Edenville goodbye. You can kiss me goodbye. All I have is this new identity. Please don't take it from me. I can't start over again." She stared up at him, letting her eyes speak.

She had powerful eyes that seemed to have the ability to express things that words couldn't. They were the eyes of a broken-hearted person, and anyone with an ounce of empathy couldn't resist their pull. She didn't flash them often, she never wanted them to become too familiar or to lose their effect, but right now they were necessary. She could tell her stare was creating small fractures in the shield Bobby had placed between them, but it had yet to shatter.

"I'm a police officer, Piper. You can't ask me to withhold information about an active case. There's a massive internal investigation going on right now. People are being linked to Judge Lions, and everyone is on edge. Edenville has been completely turned on its head, and we need to be as forthcoming as possible with any information we have. Heads are rolling, jobs are being lost, and people are going to jail. We need to stay on the right side of this. I know when you sat in your living room and told me who you really were you didn't imagine it would ever come to this. You told me because you love me, and now I'm asking you to trust me."

"Bobby, honestly, what's your hang up? You love me. That should come first. I get the good guy thing. I even understand the sense of duty, but does that really trump how you feel about me?" Piper didn't want to appear hurt, but she couldn't understand why he towed this line with so much damn conviction. What was really keeping him from putting her first?

He wanted to shout that she *didn't* understand, that maybe she never would. His own history had created that black and white definition of the world. Just as hers had made her jaded and skeptical, his past had made him this way. All he had to do was keep walking the straight and narrow to keep his demons stuffed away. The rules were the rules for a reason, and as long as he followed them he'd never find himself back in that terrible place he'd escaped. He was convinced Piper didn't need to know why he was so inflexible and law-abiding. She just needed to know and accept that he was.

When he didn't answer she continued her plea. "All I'm asking is for you to let the investigation play out for a couple of days. Let the forensic team do its job." She moved back toward him and wrapped her arms around his waist, begging him again with her eyes. "Please, promise me you'll give it a couple of days."

Bobby couldn't do that. The conflict raging inside his body kept his mouth from agreeing to her terms. He wouldn't make that promise. It was far too similar to one he'd made before, one that ended so badly he still couldn't forgive himself. "And what about everyone upstairs?" he asked as he deflected her request. "Do you plan to keep them cut out of all this? Do you want to go back to hiding everything about yourself from people who care about you?"

Piper assumed she'd need to make some kind of concession. She was asking a lot of Bobby, likely too much. It was only fair to expect she would have to give something in return. "I'm going to tell them the truth. I trust them, and I know they care about me. They deserve to know who I am." She stood on her tiptoes and held Bobby's face in her hands. "I'm sorry I'm not normal. I hate that I come with all this baggage. Please, stand by me on this."

He leaned down and kissed her, instantly calming every jagged nerve and untying all the knots in her stomach. The effect on Bobby was slightly different. The kiss didn't calm him, it scared him. Loving her scared him. She made him walk a fine line he'd always avoided. He was afraid loving her would be his undoing.

Their bodies however didn't seemed to be as conflicted as their minds. They leaned into each other, Bobby's hand grasping firmly to Piper's lower back and pulling her in tighter. There were some things that weren't impacted by the reality of a situation, and their physical attraction hadn't tapered off at all. On the contrary, the tension between their bodies, the desperate hunger to finally come together, had grown to an almost unmanageable level. She let her body grind slightly into his and a low moan passed from his mouth to hers. The passing of a rumbling motorcycle broke them from each other, reminding them that no matter how badly they wanted to give in to their desires, once again they would have to wait. Understanding the attack today would need to come first. Just like they had put the task of taking down the judge before their passion. It felt like the right thing to do at the time, but now as their bodies ached for each other and more problems stood in their way, they were both wondering if waiting had been the right choice.

Chapter Two

MICHAEL STOOD WITH his elbows on his kitchen counter, lost in a nagging thought. He couldn't believe what a weak son of a bitch he had become. He was astonished at how far he had fallen in the last few weeks. Somehow everything he once thought to be important was taking a back seat. He had worked hard to convince himself that the perfect formula for life was being a great lawyer, remaining a happy bachelor, and limiting his connections to acquaintances rather than friends. That was, of course, until he met a ragtag team of overzealous do-gooders.

In matter of weeks, they had turned him into a vigilante who had a strong allegiance to warm and fuzzy friendships. In their defense, the vigilantism had resulted in a very successful endeavor to remove a crooked judge from the bench. He took pride in the part he'd played in that. But these people were challenging everything he believed in. Take Bobby, for instance, the rookie cop with impossibly high standards for morality. It was admirable really, but at some point even Michael found his inflexible views of right and wrong unrealistic.

Making matters even more complicated was Piper, the broken girl Michael just couldn't stop trying to piece back together. She was like a shattered window, a pile of glass, all shards and slivers. You just look at it not knowing where to start. When you do finally make a plan to clean it up, all you get for your trouble is an overwhelming feeling of how insurmountable the task is, and lots of little cuts.

Then there was Betty, the diner waitress whose home-cooked meals were as warm and welcoming as her southern charm. The kitchen was an extension of her body, her pots and pans as familiar as limbs, her apron a second skin. She was a firecracker. Michael didn't think he had ever heard her whisper. She preferred to deliver impassioned soliloquys and southern idioms whenever appropriate. Hell, forget appropriate. She didn't let little things like political correctness or sensitivity to timing stop her from telling someone they were as useful as a hole in a canoe. Her words weren't merely spoken, they were delivered, infused with so much passion and feverish movements of her hands that when she got on a roll it was best to duck to avoid a finger in the eye.

To date, Michael's favorite was a comment she'd made about him. Betty, though big in personality, wasn't more than five feet and a couple inches tall whereas Michael stood a full foot over her. When chatting one day over a meatloaf with the whole gang, Michael revealed that he had been a bit on the scrawny side as a child. In an effort to make himself look taller in middle school he'd begun spiking his hair. Instead of fooling his classmates, his hair only earned him the name Spikey Mikey. God forbid he rode his bike to school, because his classmates had written a whole song about how Spikey Mikey rides his bikey. It was all rather silly, but Betty read his reminiscing as a small wound that might need a southern bandage. And what exactly was a southern bandage? Laughter.

"Michael you'd sure show those boys now if they ever saw you. Why, you're so tall if you fell down you'd be halfway home." It had sent Michael into an uncontrolled laughing fit that had him gasping for breath and leaving the table. That was the thing about Betty, she knew what joke would make you laugh, what lecture would straighten your ass out, and what kind of hug would make you feel whole on days you didn't think you could take another step. Michael wasn't a touchy feely kind of guy, but for some reason when Betty stretched her arms out he felt drawn to her like a moth to a flame.

And Betty's daughter, the redhead Jules, was another story all together. The girl was like a southern belle with the temper of a drunken sailor. She was the oddest combination of gorgeous and terrifying that he had ever encountered. They argued about the most trivial things from what super power would be the most useful in everyday life to why baked potatoes were better than mashed. They drove each other crazy, but regardless of how heated their debates, it always ended the same way. An innuendo spoken in a breathy voice, the running of a hand across a thigh, or passionate kisses broken long enough for one to declare himself or herself right about the nonsense dispute. And then hours of lovemaking that acted like a bucket of water over the fire of their argument. He didn't want to admit it, and he would most certainly deny it if asked, but they worked.

He and Jules were different enough to keep things exciting but compatible enough to enjoy each other. And though she didn't seem to realize it, Jules was the best lover Michael had ever had. It wasn't a mysterious technique or a particular fetish that made her paramount, it was her confidence, although he didn't want to discount her magnificent skills either. She had honed in on what drove him wild, what brought him to the brink, and she constantly delivered. Jules knew who she was, what she liked, and what she wanted. She didn't waver, which at times made her infuriatingly stubborn and hotheaded, but it also meant he didn't need to think for her, something he hated to have to do.

So often women in his life became passengers, ready to go where he took them, ready to accept what he would give, but Jules set her own standard for happiness and had her own idea of life. The fact that she appealed to him in every way had landed him in unfamiliar territory. She could keep up with him in a heated debate and in bed. That combination was hard to find. He liked girls who were easy to walk away from, forgettable girls. Jules was anything but forgettable. Even now, in a room full of other people and at a safe distance from each other, he found it difficult to control his arousal. It took only the passing hint of her savory perfume or a sideways glance as she nibbled her bottom lip to send him into a calming chant.

Baseball, Mrs. Gobelstone from third grade with the mustache, spiders crawling in your ears—all usually sure-fire ways to dampen the excitement that grew in him whenever they were close.

Now, as he moved to his living room, readying himself to hear whatever sordid tale Piper was about to share, Michael realized his time with these people was probably far from over. He could read the grave expression on Piper's face. That, paired with the fact that Bobby had insisted all three women come to his house to be safe, let him know this was something significant. And the only thing about that revelation that bothered him was he felt relieved. Why on earth was he happy that another crazy force was about to thrust him even closer to all of them? He should feel suffocated and annoyed, but all he could think was maybe this would extend their connection. Having more time with people who made him finally feel like he was a part of something left him uncharacteristically soothed.

Suddenly Betty's sweet southern voice cut in, interrupting Michael's internal battle. She'd spent the day busying herself around his tiny kitchen, which was her favorite room in any house. "Oh, where are my manners—thank you, Michael, for inviting us to stay in your home... or loft? I'm not sure what you call a place like this." He could tell from her expression that she clearly couldn't appreciate his decorating style.

Jules, who was often embarrassed by her mother's inability to enjoy things she didn't understand, waved her hand trying to quiet her mother. "Ma, don't act like that. It's a great place. It's just different than you're used to. I'm sure he's fixing to put curtains up eventually." If she were honest with herself, Jules agreed that the apartment was awful. Everything seemed to be made of steel, brick, or glass. There wasn't a single picture or knick-knack anywhere. But she was enthusiastic in her attempts to appreciate Michael's unique decorating style, which she had concluded could be described as "bachelor minimalist."

"I wasn't trying to be ugly about it. I'm just not sure what I'm sitting on here," Betty snickered, adjusting herself on the rigid bar stool where she was perched.

"It's ergonomic," Michael answered, not daring to tell her it cost five hundred dollars. He wasn't dumb enough to engage in that debate. Jules tried hard to change the subject before Betty could break into a story about furniture styles from her childhood. "Piper has something to tell us," Jules said quickly, her motives clear. "Go ahead, Piper."

Piper waved them over to the living room and they all joined her. "This isn't something that's easy for me to talk about," Piper started, as Jules and Betty sat by her on the couch. It was black leather with sharp wood edges and offered no clear way to get comfortable. Bobby and Michael sat across from them in two large leather recliners.

"We're all here for you, Piper," Betty said, squeezing her thigh, ironically close to where the jagged number twenty-three had been carved into her skin.

"I won't give you all the gory details. The short version: I didn't grow up in a very good home. My parents weren't like you." She hesitated, resting her head on Betty's shoulder for a moment. "I grew up in Brooklyn, and every day was a struggle. Through the help of a priest, my mother and I finally broke away from my father, who was a very violent man."

Michael watched as Piper fought back her nerves. After a long moment of silence she shook her head and turned toward Bobby. With her eyes, she begged him to step in.

Understanding her pleading look, Bobby continued for her. "Piper's real name is Isabella. It was changed after her father hunted them down. He attacked them, and her mother didn't survive. Piper barely did. The way he killed Piper's mother and tried to kill Piper was very specific. It drew the attention of the FBI. When Piper was recovering, they came in and told her she'd been attacked by a person they had dubbed the Railway Killer. They knew this because he used the same weapon and techniques every time he killed someone. That's when Piper realized her dad wasn't just a violent guy who treated his family badly. He was responsible for over twenty murders." Bobby left out the part that ate at Piper's conscience the most. How she had stayed silent for weeks after her own attack in an effort to ignore the truth.

That hesitation on her part resulted in the murder of another girl at the hands of her father. She held her breath as Bobby continued. "Piper was placed in witness protection, and that's how she ended up here in Edenville." Michael was glad Piper was sitting next to Betty and Jules instead of having to see their reaction head on as he did. Instead, she locked eyes with Michael who purposefully clenched his jaw, keeping his face impassive. He was a steady guy, not overly emotional. He knew he could offer some composure.

"I know that case," Michael interjected. "We studied it in law school, and I've followed it over the years. The Railway Killer has one of the most methodical and ritualistic styles of killing in recent history. There's been no activity from him in over two years. The chatter was he must have died. No one with that type of compulsion just falls off the radar."

"The girl attacked this morning..." Piper trembled, not looking ready to admit this out loud, "she had a mark on her leg similar to what my father left on me. It's what he leaves on all his victims. But there was so much about the attack this morning that doesn't align with his murders. We really can't be certain there's anything to worry about yet."

Jules had a look of bewilderment on her face and Michael worried that she may ask something Piper wasn't ready to answer. He'd spent plenty of time around victims and understood the sensitivity required. Jules tended to have a more direct approach with things in her life and it concerned him in these moments.

"What do you mean, he 'marked' you?" she asked looking over Piper's body as if she had missed some kind of telltale sign of a killer. Michael watched as Piper hesitated to answer, and clearly saw that Bobby wasn't sure exactly how to broach the subject either. These seemed like the details Piper didn't want to relive again.

Michael saw the uncomfortable glances passing between Bobby and Piper and decided to switch over to his prosecutor persona. There was a way to eliminate the emotion, the personal weight of the conversation, and he knew how to do that well. "The Railway Killer uses a sharpened railroad spike to sever the femoral artery of his victims. He then carves that victim's number into their upper thigh with a small knife. What Piper is saying, is when her father tried to kill her he carved a number in her leg, and I'm guessing the girl attacked on campus must have had something similar."

Jules's eyes instinctively fixed on Piper's leg. Michael could almost hear the questions fluttering through her mind. What number was it? Did it hurt? He watched as she bit at her lip to stay silent.

Betty clasped her hand around Piper's and eyed Jules to do the same. As the three women sat with their hands together, Michael felt a warm feeling in his chest. He'd seen so many victims who had to stand alone, it was comforting to see someone with a soft place to fall. He turned toward Bobby and asked what he thought was an obvious question. "What did the police say? Are the FBI already on scene?"

"They haven't made any connection to my father yet," Piper said, attempting to sound casual, as if Michael might actually let it go.

"Are you going down to talk to them tonight? You have to tell them who you are and what you know." Michael sat up a little straighter in his seat, readying himself for a war of words if it came to that.

"The girl attacked today had the number twenty-three carved in her leg. It doesn't even make sense," Piper boomed defiantly, startling Betty and Jules who jumped slightly. "He didn't try to kill her, there was no wound to her femoral artery. The information about my father is available to anyone with Internet access. This could easily be a copycat, or a rogue crazy person just trying to feel connected to the case. I've read hundreds of websites over the years dedicated to my father. He has fan clubs. The second I expose myself, my life in Edenville is over. The FBI will swoop in here and Piper Anderson won't exist anymore."

"And every second you don't tell them who you are, you're unprotected. You can't roll the dice on this being some kind of coincidence," Michael shouted, meeting her raised voice with his own.

"I'm not saying I won't come forward, I'm just saying let's give it a couple of days for more information to come out. Let them go over the evidence before we do something we can't take back." Piper let her voice drop from angry to scared. "I'm not ready to leave here."

Betty put her hand to Piper's cheek and rubbed it gently. "There isn't a man on this earth, government agent or killer, who is going to take you from us. I'm sorry you never had much family, but you have one now. We can get through this together." She shot a threatening look over to Bobby and Michael, letting them know the subject was closed for now.

"Thank you, Betty." Piper let the tears forming in her eyes spill over. Michael reluctantly realized Betty was the only one speaking with her heart. He wished he could offer the same but it just wasn't logical in this situation.

Michael blew out an exasperated breath and looked over at Bobby as if to question *are we really agreeing to this?* Bobby shrugged back at him looking equally as conflicted but, at the same time, helpless. "A couple of days," Michael said, resignedly shaking his head. "But we act as though this is your father. We take all the necessary precautions for your safety, for everyone's safety."

"I know this is a lot to take in all at once," Piper stuttered, rubbing the tears from her eyes and looking at each of them. "This chaos has been a part of my life for as long as I can remember, but this is the first time I haven't been alone." She smiled gratefully and Michael's heart ached for her.

"Michael, I want to ask you something," Piper said quietly.

"Of course," he replied. "You can ask me anything." He

couldn't think of a single thing he wouldn't do for her at this point, and frankly that worried him.

"What the hell is wrong with your apartment?" She kept the same deadpan look on her face as she spoke. "It's like a combination of a sterilized operating room and a cave. How do you live like this?" She let her face break into a smile as Betty let out a loud cackle and Jules brought her hand to her mouth to stifle her giggle. Michael couldn't help but smirk. He enjoyed how, even in the darkest moments, this group could still find small pieces of joy. He'd overlook the fact they were at his expense.

He wasn't, however, going to take this lying down. "Have you people never heard of Modernism? Just because we're in North Carolina doesn't mean everything has to be rustic and well-worn. That couch you're sitting on is a one-of-a-kind. It cost me two months' pay." His face was red as he gestured over to his furniture.

"Well you got screwed!" Piper exclaimed. "I feel like I'm sitting on a piece of driftwood wrapped in leather. Next time you go furniture shopping remember this—rule number one: the couch shouldn't be *sharp*."

He rolled his eyes and shook his head now that the whole room was laughing at his designing skills. "I'm sorry, next time I'll make sure to run over to Goodwill and get the fluffiest dust-mite-collecting plaid couch they have."

"See if they have any curtains, or maybe something that isn't made out of metal." Piper was laughing now, and though Michael didn't like being the butt of the joke he was happy to see her having fun. Jules and Betty were on either side of her, their bodies shuddering with amusement. When they composed themselves for even a moment one would point to the odd steel lamp with clear plastic shade or the spirally spindles carved into the edges of his coffee table and laughter would begin again.

Michael looked over at Bobby who was being far more polite than the girls. Still, he couldn't help making one small quip. Bobby fought back the urge to laugh as he spoke, "I like it, it's all very *you*."

With that, the girls all spilled over onto one another, hooting away. Betty calmed herself long enough to make a request. "Can we please just move this bookcase? It's blocking that beautiful bay window. You'd get so much more natural light. You have to start somewhere."

Bobby and Michael obediently rose and started taking commands from all three women who were still sitting on the couch. They pointed and shouted as Michael and Bobby shifted furniture to the left three inches, then back to the right. They squared themselves up to move the large mahogany bookcase as they waited for the girls to decide on its new and improved location.

"Make up your minds," Michael demanded. "I'm moving this thing once. It's heavy as hell and I'm not throwing my back out because you can't agree." When they finally chose the perfect spot, Bobby and Michael began shimmying and shoving it in that direction. It snagged on the throw rug and Michael wedged himself in behind it, squeezing between the wall and the bookcase. His intention was to tilt it back toward himself so Bobby could move the carpet out of the way. But when he tried to move his arms, he realized the space was much smaller than he'd anticipated. As he went to slip himself out, Bobby's maneuvering closed Michael in further.

"Can you tilt it back?" Bobby asked putting all his weight into trying to lean it toward Michael.

"I'd love to, if I could move my damn arms. I'm stuck." He pushed at it with his shoulder but the carpet was bunching beneath it and keeping it from budging. When they all began to realize that Michael was in fact wedged quite tightly behind the bookcase they couldn't help but find the humor in it, though Michael certainly wasn't enjoying it.

"Would you ladies please get off your asses and help move this? I'm starting to feel like Baby Jessica in the well back here."

Bobby, Jules, and Piper all looked at each other blankly.

"Who is Baby Jessica?" Jules asked, her voice laced with confusion.

"Seriously?" Michael shouted from behind the bookcase. "You people don't know who Baby Jessica is? I need to start hanging out with people my own age, you can't appreciate good eighties references." There were less than ten years between all of them but these were the moments Michael realized what a difference a decade could make.

"I'm sure my mom knows what you're talking about. You guys will always be able to tell your old-timer jokes to each other." Jules peeked into the small space where Michael was standing and he growled at her.

"Just shut up and put your hundred ten pounds into moving this stupid thing." As they all worked to free him, Michael caught a glimpse of Piper giggling with Jules. He realized this might just be a normal moment of joking for anyone else, but for Piper this was probably what she'd been missing all these years. Now all they had to do was make sure she stayed alive long enough to enjoy it.

Chapter Three

THEY HAD ALL become a little too good at altering their lives for safety purposes. When they were trying to take down the judge and the risk to them was greatest, they'd found ways to make it all work. It wasn't something they wanted to be so practiced at, but they were practically professionals now. Once again, they adjusted their schedules and sleeping arrangements to ensure strength in numbers. Piper had taken an open-ended leave from the cable company. She told them she had a personal issue, and, surprisingly, they had been supportive. They let her know that if there was a position available when she was ready to return, it would be hers. If they had only known how frequently she had used her position at CableCom to gain entrance into people's homes in order to further her own agenda, they certainly wouldn't be so accommodating. She later heard through the grapevine that her employment there was a crucial part of a "diversity" initiative. Apparently, though she wasn't surprised after the way she had been received by most customers, CableCom had trouble attracting and keeping female employees in Edenville.

Jules and Michael had aligned their shifts so that he dropped her off and picked her up each day at Town Hall. It was certainly convenient since they were all staying at Betty's house. Bobby and Piper had taken over the two couches in the sitting room while Michael had begun sleeping upstairs with Jules in her childhood room. She had put most of her belongings in storage after her annulment from Scott, hoping it wouldn't be long before she was moving into a new apartment. Her old bedroom unfortunately still had all its pink ruffles and a tiny bed, which made the experience not only physically uncomfortable, but a little psychologically disconcerting as well.

Life at Betty's house was definitely cramped. Yes, the meals were amazing, the conversation lively, the company wonderful, but the space was small. Michael, Bobby, and Piper sat quietly on the front porch taking refuge from the confined quarters and enjoying the midafternoon sun. The weather had turned colder, but there were still days, if the sun was shining brightly, when you could easily forget it was almost winter.

Bobby read the worried look on Piper's face as she stared out to the end of the driveway. "What is it, Piper?" he asked, reaching over to hold her hand. They were back on their swing, the place they'd first fallen in love. She shook herself out of her thoughts and took comfort in the fact that Bobby's hand, warm and encompassing, still felt as thrilling today as the first time she had held it. It was such a small act of intimacy, but when you have no privacy, you take what you can get. She was frequently surprising herself lately. Her thoughts would get away from her and before she knew it she'd be picturing the two of them writhing in pleasure, his eyes locked on hers. Something, a crack of reality, would make its way back in and she'd realize that she'd been quiet too long, or that eyes were on her. Her cheeks would pink and she'd fight to squelch the heat rising in her.

"I'm grateful for everything you guys are doing for me, but it feels extreme. There isn't really enough room for all of us to stay here. Aren't you getting a little sick of it?"

"I'm with you, Piper," Michael said, exhaling dramatically and cutting in before Bobby could reply. "I'm not sure I can go too many more nights sleeping in that pretty princess room. There isn't much privacy in this house. The walls are paper thin, and Thumbelina's bed up there squeaks like a rusty hinge. Let's just say it's not really setting the mood right now. I'd imagine the two lumpy couches in the sitting room aren't cutting it for you two either. Maybe we should consider splitting up. There's no reason you and Piper can't go stay at your place for a night, and the next night Jules and I can stay at my place. I care about you, Piper, but a man has his limits."

Piper wanted to walk over and high-five the man. He hadn't sugarcoated it or danced around the issue. They were all grown people, who, since meeting, hadn't had nearly enough time alone. She and Bobby barely had a chance to kiss passionately before someone would be coming in to chat or walk by to fill a late-night glass of water from the kitchen. Piper sat up a little straighter, and, out of painfully obvious desperation, shouted, "Yes!"

At that, Michael let out a laugh. "I guess you guys should take the first night then. At least Jules and I have a door. Sure there's a sticker on it that warns *no boys allowed*, but that's a loosely followed guideline."

Bobby was reluctant, but he had to admit, a night alone with Piper wasn't just tempting, it was impossible to turn down. It took fewer than thirty minutes for Bobby and Piper to stuff clothes into their duffle bags and say their goodbyes. They hadn't talked details, they had no set plans, but they weren't going to let that slow them down. They both sank with a sigh of relief into the cab of Bobby's truck. They waved farewell to their three friends who were perched on the porch. Betty was waving her normal gentle goodbye while Jules and Michael were giggling to each other, seeming to mock Bobby and Piper's hurry to leave. They'd apparently done a feeble job at hiding their desperation for each other.

Bobby turned on the radio softly, and Piper could hear a familiar country song humming through the speakers. "Where should we go, your place or mine?" he asked, knowing how much that sounded like a pick-up line best saved for a bar.

She didn't care about the cheesy line. As a matter of fact she didn't care if they never spoke another word again until they were exhausted from passion. They had been patient, they had leapt every obstacle and waited for the right time, but now Piper was becoming more convinced that if they didn't seize the moment, the right time would never come.

"You've already seen my place. It's nothing special. I'm very curious about your apartment. Maybe we should go there." She imagined his place to be the ultimate bachelor pad. Maybe the end tables would be milk crates and the bed frame made of cinder blocks.

"It's not really an apartment," Bobby admitted, blushing a little. That reaction sent Piper's imagination into overdrive.

"Is it a trailer?" she asked, trying not to sound put off by the idea. The apartments of her youth were nothing to brag about. There were frequently more cockroaches than tenants.

"No," he said, snickering a bit at her assumption. "It's a house. When my parents moved back up north a couple of years ago I moved into an apartment. I couldn't settle in though, it all felt temporary. So I bought a little house on the edge of town. It isn't far from your place. It's just set back in the County Grove neighborhood."

They drove in silence for the next few minutes as they entered the beautifully landscaped neighborhood. The sun seemed to shine brighter around these houses, and there was a wonderful sense of community here. Children were playing in the yards, neighbors chatting by the mailbox.

Piper frequently found herself resisting the urge to imagine life after all this mess with her father was over. She wasn't one to be overly optimistic or to dream of better days. She preferred reality. But as they pulled up to Bobby's charming little blue house with its pristinely landscaped yard and intricately carved front door, she heard her heart say, *I could see us living here. We could make a life in this house.* Bobby pulled into the stone driveway and parked. In his usual gentlemanly fashion, he crossed in front of the truck and made his way to Piper's door. He pulled it open and Piper realized this was something that would never get old. They locked hands as they moved up his front walk, and as much as she continued to try to fight it, she felt like she was walking into her future.

When he turned the key in the door Piper's mind was twirling with excitement, alight with images of a thousand tomorrows. As she entered and scanned the room, she couldn't help but shake her head in disbelief.

"What's the matter?" Bobby asked, squirming a little and looking self-conscious about his space and her reaction to it. She searched the living room for the smallest sign of mismatched furniture or sports memorabilia. When her search turned up nothing, she turned to face Bobby. The couches were sand-colored suede with matching warm-toned pillows. The room was bordered with white trim that popped against the subtle blue walls. Framed art hung symmetrically above the mantle. The whole place was warm and inviting and was in stark contrast to not only Michael's place but also to how Piper imagined it would look.

"Where's the lopsided old microwave cart you're supposed to have your television on? Where's the coffee table you made yourself out of pallets? I don't see a single sports magazine anywhere. This house looks like something a grown-up would live in," she teased as she gestured over her shoulder to his things.

"We *are* grown-ups," he whispered, reaching toward her and tucking a loose lock of hair behind her ear, implying they were about to partake in some very adult activities. She narrowed her eyes at him knowing something was up. He broke their locked gaze and dropped his head in embarrassment. "All right, you caught me. I bought all of this in one shopping trip. This was exactly how it was set up at Houston's Furniture Store, and I told them to wrap it all up, right down to the coasters. I did the same thing for the kitchen and bedroom." Piper wanted to engage him in banter about how ridiculous it was to buy full sets of furniture from a place like that. The vase on the table was pretty, but it had probably cost him significantly more from a furniture store than it would have anywhere else. But she said none of that. Her mind had gotten hung up on the mention of his bedroom, the thought of them in his bed.

"Do you want something to drink?" he stammered, now looking suddenly uncomfortable by her silence. This wasn't at all how she imagined this would go. She thought they'd be down to their socks by now, tripping over each other as they raced for the bedroom, but Bobby looked hesitant. They were clearly not on the same wavelength, because Piper's body was full of hot tingling pressure with not the least bit of doubt about what they should be doing right now. Maybe, this isn't what he wanted. Maybe she read things wrong.

"No thanks," she replied disappointedly. As he moved past her their bodies brushed against one another and it took all of her willpower not to grab him. It sent a shock through her, but he kept moving toward the kitchen. The floor plan was open, so Piper could see right in as Bobby pulled open his fridge and reached for a beer. He spun open the top and flipped it into the trash. He took a long swig, and as he finished he leaned himself against the counter and sighed.

"What are you doing?" Piper asked with a huff.

"What do you mean, I'm having a drink. I asked you if you wanted one. Do you?" Bobby replied, confused by her attitude.

"No, I don't want a beer. Did we come here to hydrate? Maybe I missed something, but we've been holed up with a bunch of people, *dying* to be alone together. Now here we are and you're just standing there." Her hands were on her hips now. She was starting to feel like maybe her desire for him was much stronger than his for her. And for a person like Piper, that was unsettling.

"I didn't want you to think I was some kind of animal. I figured maybe you wanted to talk for a bit." Bobby looked stunned by her flash of anger. She knew he was usually the one pouring his heart out, always reassuring her of his feelings. She could tell by the crooked smile breaking across his face that he was happy for the role reversal. He looked glad to see her so desperate for him.

"You're a gentleman. You open doors, you pay for meals, you say please and thank you. I love that about you. It's really charming. But right now, I could use a little less of that. No, a lot less of that. Every time we get anywhere close to having our moment, something happens. I'm tired of it. I want to be with you now. Right *now*." She punctuated the words purposefully to make herself entirely clear, and continued in a frustrated voice. "I don't care if the phone rings or an asteroid hits the earth. I don't need chivalry—I need to be in your bed, with next to no clothes on, finding ways to forget how awful my life is right now. Do you think you can do that?" Her face was red, half with embarrassment and half with anger, and her hands remained perched on her hips.

Bobby raised his eyebrows as his lips curled into a playful smile. This was certainly a side of Piper he had never seen before. He had wanted her for so long and repeatedly fought his body's relentless cues to take her. Now, here he was alone with her, permission fully granted, and he was completely ready.

He put his beer down on the counter. He moved with such intention, such confidence, that her hands dropped from her hips, and she suddenly felt nervous. It was all finally about to happen, and maybe she wasn't as ready as she thought she was.

But when his lips met hers and his sturdy arms pulled her body in against his, she knew it was time, and she could clearly feel he was ready, too. He backed her up against the front door and kissed her with a hunger that had been a long time coming. His tongue explored her mouth; his hands ran anxiously through her hair. He was answering her question without saying a word. He was ready to please her. He was ready to make her forget.

They moved around the room, sparks seeming to fly from them. They went from the couch to the kitchen, making their way to the bedroom clumsily, as neither wanted to release the other as they moved. Bobby pulled his shirt over his head, and a burst of his scent filled Piper's nose. The perfect mix of fresh soap and sheer masculinity and it was driving her wild.

She felt her nerves flare, but tried to keep them in check. She wasn't just bothered by the length of time that passed since she'd last had sex; she'd never had sex with someone she loved. Sex had been a means to an end, an event, not a connection. What would it be like to lock eyes with Bobby as he moved inside her? How would it feel to lie in his arms when they had both finished, paralyzed by pleasure and exhaustion? Could she really give herself over to him like that? She wasn't sure, but she was dying to find out.

She hastily pulled at the buttons on her shirt and felt one come loose and fall to the floor. She didn't care, she could sew it back on, she could buy a new shirt, she could burn it, nothing was going to slow them down. When all the buttons were finally free, she shook the shirt off her shoulders. Bobby stopped kissing her and pulled away. They were in the hallway now, just steps from his bedroom and he wanted to see her. He looked down at her body, remembering the only other time he had seen her perfect caramel skin wrapped in the fancy lace of her bra. He smiled at the memory, at how far they had come from that day in the town hall office when he'd accidentally walked in on her changing.

He pulled her back in and deepened the kiss, sending an excited rush through her body. His hands slid down, found the back of her thighs, and he lifted her up in one swift motion. She straddled him, wrapping her legs around his waist as he carried her into his room.

She wanted to be lost in the passion of the moment, but a quick survey of his room left her giggling. "You bought the decorative fake plant from the furniture store, too? Seriously, no one buys that."

He rolled his eyes and tossed her onto his bed, appreciating her joke but not letting it slow him down. He towered over her now, and she felt his hand on the button of her pants. Her face grew serious and she placed her hand over his.

"I know you've seen my scar before, but I haven't been with anyone since it happened. I just thought you should know." She was looking away from him as she spoke. She had come to accept the mark on her leg, but really she was more afraid *he* couldn't see past it. He gently removed her hand, unbuttoned her pants and moved them down off her waist, exposing the scar on her thigh as well as the black lace of her panties.

The scar did nothing to distract him from his desire to pull the rest of her clothes off, unwrapping her like a present he'd spent months waiting to open. But if it worried her, then he'd do his best to show her how insignificant it truly was. "Did you know we met on the twenty-third? That day at the diner when I chased after you, it was the twenty-third. This scar is a part of you, and I know that it isn't an easy thing to carry around, but we can make it mean whatever we want it to. He might have given it to you, but he doesn't get to tell you how to feel about it." He traced the raised number twenty-three with his finger and leaned down to kiss her again.

After a moment of indulging in the passion of his lips, she felt all her anxiety melt away. Their bodies were now moving together, the remainder of their clothes being shed like weights dropping to the ground and lightening them in a way they hadn't felt before. Being there in his arms, naked and exposed, Piper felt a chill run through her body, not a cold chill but the kind that makes its way over you before you even know it's coming. It started in her back and ended somewhere in the warmth spreading between her legs. It was a good chill, a *very good* chill. As she ran her hands up and down his chest she kept silently admiring his body, the perfection of it, the hard work it must take to maintain it.

With every new angle of his body coming into view she felt more disadvantaged. His abs were defined muscles that tightened under her touch. Her stomach was flat but not toned. His arms looked as though they were sculpted, the muscles rock hard under his skin. Her arms felt too long and out of practice for all of this. His calves and thighs had run miles today and it showed with every flex. She felt too thick in the thighs, wondered, *was a B cup enough*? She'd never been completely satisfied with her body, what woman was? Oh crap, did she really miss a spot when shaving her legs this morning? But to her surprise Bobby seemed to be perfectly thrilled with each new surface of her body he discovered, so she fought down her nagging voice of insecurity.

They moved to the top of the bed with all its matching decorative pillows and shams, probably purchased from a display window at the department store. This was what they had patiently waited for. This was their moment. He trailed light kisses down her neck and ran his thumb across her collarbone. His other hand was caught up in her silky hair, running his fingers through it again and again. As she readied herself for him, the anticipation driving her nearly to the brink, Piper heard an odd thump and pulled Bobby's body closer to hers. Maybe it was the slamming of a car door or the passing of a loud truck, maybe it was her heart thudding in her chest. Either way it unsettled her. Looking past him she exclaimed, "Bobby, your blinds are open."

He reluctantly released her earlobe from between his teeth and glanced over his shoulder. "No one can see in, it's the backyard," he assured her as their bodies separated and he stood, reaching for the cord on the blinds. She watched him standing there and took in the magnificence of his naked body. She was lightheaded with the thought of what was to come, how long it had been since she'd felt a firm grip on her hips, the pleasure of moving as one. As he made his way back to her, kneeling on the bed, he flashed a devilish smile, and she playfully backed away trying to tease him.

Suddenly, with a startling loud buzz and piercing static, a voice echoed loudly through the room. "Car BR3 what is your position? We have a possible 138 outside McCormick's Bar."

Piper jumped back in fear but was already closer to the edge of the bed than she had realized. She tumbled backward off the bed and landed with a hard thud on the floor. Bobby slapped at the box on his nightstand, silencing the shrill voice of the dispatcher. He lunged across the bed, laying on his stomach and looked down at Piper who had her head in her hands.

"Are you okay?" he asked, not able to read Piper's reaction. "I have a police scanner in here. I keep it turned up really loud so I can hear it from the living room. I forgot to turn it off." He reached his hand down toward her, and she peeked through her fingers up at him.

"I fell off the bed," she croaked, not sure if she wanted to laugh or cry.

"I can see that," he replied with a wry smile. "Do you want to come back *on* the bed?" he asked as he reached his hand down and ran his finger across her shoulder.

"No," she mumbled, too embarrassed get up. She peered through her fingers and pouted up at him. "I fell off the bed," she said again, still sounding tragically self-conscious.

He slid his body forward and braced himself with his hands in front of him on the floor. In a flash he was lying next to her on the cozy area rug that had come with his furniture. "I fell off the bed, too," he teased as he ran his finger from her toes, over her knee and up her leg. When she smiled widely at him, he knew she was all right. She lay back, welcoming him to join her. He moved on top of her, and stared down into her eyes as they became one. She drew in a raspy breath and murmured, "Finally." She didn't just mean finally they were having sex, it was more than that. She had finally let go, finally given herself to someone.

They spent the next few hours exploring the depths of their ecstasy. They slipped in and out of short restful sleep, only to wake up to the other's tantalizing caress, igniting passion once more. When their bodies gave out, their eyes too heavy to fight the comfort of sleep, they faded away together. They slept tangled in each other, legs locked together, so close they seemed to be breathing the same air. For Piper it wasn't long before the elation of their lovemaking bled into the haunting clouds of her nightmares.

Hiding—Piper was great at it. She could turn any small space into a sanctuary to try to avoid danger. It didn't always work but there was something about being tucked away in a tiny space that made her feel secure. She'd found a closet at elementary school that was meant for storing old supplies and tools, and many afternoons were spent crouched behind the large industrial garbage can in the corner. She was there, tucked behind it, her bruised knees pulled up to her chest, as the door swung open. Mr. Olivares, the new teacher, strolled to the wall and started pawing through a bucket of dried up markers.

He was a handsome young man. He had kind eyes and she liked the way he switched easily between Spanish and English. She jumped a little as he began to speak to himself. "I swear this school is such a dump. I can't even find a decent writing utensil. Por qué llegué a esta escuela?" In his frustration, as he turned away he accidently pulled the bucket down and markers rolled in every direction, one to her feet. She was frozen with fear. As Mr. Olivares gathered them his eyes found her ripped yellow sneakers, and he jumped back in fear. "Ay Dios mio! What are you doing back there?" he asked, covering his heart with his hand. "Come, come."

He led Piper to his empty classroom and set her in his large rolling desk chair. She felt powerful sitting behind his desk like a grown up; at nine years old that was still something to get excited about. Mr. Olivares looked her over. Her dirty face, her torn clothes, and her bruised legs. He'd seen this girl before but had apparently looked through her rather than at her.

"This is a safe place," he said as he crouched down in front of her. "If you are in some kind of trouble, if someone is hurting you, you can tell me. I can help you." This had never happened before. An actual grown-up had never told her they saw her and realized something was the matter, then offered to help her. She wasn't the only one in her school, not even the only one in her class, who clearly had a hard home life. The bruises weren't exclusive to her.

Sometimes when something was so prevalent, it became accepted. But Mr. Olivares was new here, he'd never seen a place like this before—he didn't know any better, so he tried to help.

Sitting silently she contemplated the idea of confessing her pain to him. He'd be horrified, he'd be disgusted, but would he help her or make it worse? This was a fork in the road; stay the course or take a chance? But then she remembered Alison

Campari. She'd been beaten badly by her mother, and rather than staying home long enough for the worst of the injuries to heal she'd come to school. The teachers couldn't ignore her eye, swollen shut and oozing pus.

Child Services was called. She was removed from her home—her mother arrested, charged, jailed. Eight weeks later Alison was on the news, near death from a violent rape at the hands of her foster father. Sometimes, even when you think it can't get much worse, it can. Sometimes bad isn't as bad as it gets. She looked into the sweet eyes of the worried teacher and smiled. She wouldn't tell him a thing. She'd make up a story about the girls in gym class picking on her, that she was sad and wanted to hide. She'd roll the dice that whatever was out there waiting for her might be worse than what was at home.

But that gamble didn't always pay off. That night she'd managed to do her homework in spite of the blaring music her father was listening to as he slipped in and out of a drunken stupor. She heard a knock on her door and panic filled her. This wasn't the type of place people dropped by to visit; they weren't the kind of people who ever had company.

Her mother shook awake her father, who was slouched over on the couch. "Did you pay Marty?" she asked, waving for Piper to sit still and be silent. "Huh?" her father groaned. "Yeah, I paid him today." The knock came again, this time slightly louder. "Go get the damn door," he said shoving his wife away from him. She tried to smooth down the matted parts of her brassy bleached hair and straighten her wrinkled shirt.

Her mother pulled open the door and there stood a very timid looking Mr. Olivares. His hands were folded behind his back, his eyes trying hard to shine in the face of the horror he had seen walking through the building that was littered with trash.

Now standing in the doorway looking at another travesty he'd only imagined before today, he spoke. "Hello, my name is Mr. Olivares. I'm a teacher at your daughter's school. She had a tough day today and I just wanted to check in and make sure *she was doing okay."*

Her mother's head spun around and daggers shot from her eyes at her daughter who was trying hard to hide her fear. She wasn't sure what was more frightening, Mr. Olivares discovering her horrible secrets or leaving without discovering them.

"I'm fine," she managed to croak out at the urging of her mother's glare. Her father was now pulling himself to an upright position and joining the conversation.

"They let wetbacks teach now? What's this world coming to?" He managed to stand and stroll uneasily over to the door where Mr. Olivares now stood with wide, fear-filled eyes. Her father could have that effect on people. He had characteristics of a monster that he could flash whenever he liked, turning them on and off as needed. "I'm guessing you were trying to catch my little girl home alone, huh? You thought maybe you could have a little fun with her?"

"No," Mr. Olivares replied, his face twisted in confusion and disgust. "I can assure you that was not my intention. She had a rough day at school and I wanted to make sure you were aware of it and that she was feeling better. That was all."

"Well, we're aware of it now," snapped her mother, slamming the door in his face. Both her parents spun around and their eyes bore into her. She'd broken a cardinal rule. She'd brought attention to this house. That was not allowed. There would be hell to pay. As the dream turned into a reliving of the brutal beating she'd endured that day, her body couldn't help but react.

Piper shoved at Bobby's arm that had been resting comfortably over her shoulder, and she pulled her hands up over her face, protecting it as she had from her parents' blows. She drew her legs up, forcing her body into the smallest version of herself. As Bobby woke, finding Piper cowering next to him in bed, he searched the room, expecting to find some tangible danger. Then as he looked her over once more he realized she was asleep, fighting some kind of evil he couldn't see.

"Piper," he boomed, reaching down and putting his hand on her shoulder and shaking her slightly. Piper's arm shot up reflexively, her elbow connecting sharply with the skin above his eye and causing him to reel backwards in shock. The impact of her arm on real flesh rather than the ghosts of her dreams had Piper shooting up in bed, panting and trembling.

She searched the room for Bobby who had tumbled off the bed and was currently rubbing the spot above his eye that she'd nailed with her elbow.

"I'm sorry," she said, shifting herself in bed to get a better look at him. "I was dreaming, I didn't mean to hit you."

"I think falling out of bed every time we have sex isn't a habit we should get into. People are going to start talking." He climbed back up to the bed and she examined his eye, marked red but not bleeding or swelling. "What were you dreaming about?" he asked, rubbing her cold shoulder with his warm hand.

She thought about it for a minute. She considered how conflicted Mr. Olivares must have been, how scared he probably was that day. He'd never really looked at her again. They never spoke about any of it. When she'd come in the following day, fresh bruises on her arm, he'd ignored them, and she let him. Welcomed it really. She didn't blame Mr. Olivares for his decision.

Piper now realized that he had been younger than she was now. He'd probably never seen anything like the world she grew up in, and maybe he just couldn't find a way to justify the risk. He was one of dozens who stood by and quietly ignored the epidemic in her school. His complacency was nothing more than self-preservation, and she had forgiven him.

Escaping her own mind, she decided answering Bobby's question with the level of detail he wanted wasn't what she needed right now. "Hell," she whispered leaning into him for a hug. "I was dreaming about hell." She had truly come through hell to get to this moment. But at least tonight, she'd been able to glimpse heaven.

Chapter Four

PIPER KEPT ENCOUNTERING moments that felt like they should be memories from another time in her life. Things she'd never experienced, but should have. Betty would occasionally do something overtly maternal like pack her a lunch in a brown bag for when she'd spend the day at work with Michael. There would be a paper napkin folded inside with an encouraging note written in Betty's swirling scrawl. A few days ago while Piper was sitting on the floor watching television, without saying a word, Betty sat on the couch behind her and began braiding her hair. Betty acted as if it was the most natural thing in the world. And in that moment, to Piper, it felt like it was. She wasn't sure if a person could play catch-up, if you could backfill all the things you had missed in your life, but she figured it didn't hurt to try.

Now, sitting on the floor of Jules's room and listening to music while they painted their nails, Piper knew she was taking part in another missed moment. It didn't hurt that the ambiance of the room, with all its pink ruffles and heartthrob posters, transported them back to feeling like teenagers again.

"Do you think I'm easy?" Jules asked as she blew on her wet nails, glowing with fresh red polish.

"Do you mean easy as in promiscuous?" Piper replied nervously, not prepared for this question. Up until this point they had been casually gabbing about television shows they liked.

"Yes. Do you think what I'm doing with Michael makes me look easy? You and Bobby haven't been together long, but at least you know you love each other. I can't even figure out if Michael and I would be together if he didn't feel like he had to be here to protect me. He never talks about his feelings, so I sure as hell don't want to be the one to say anything. Maybe that makes me stupid for keeping this up." Jules reached for the polish and touched up one of her nails as she spoke.

"If I had to judge you by your nail polish colors here I would say yes, you must be easy. Who names these things? *Pop my Cherry Red* and *Morning After Mauve,* are they serious? Good thing these aren't the same people responsible for naming crayons." Piper tipped each bottle over, reading the labels, amazed by the innuendo the companies were able to get away with. "You and Michael are two grown, single people who aren't hurting anyone else. I don't think what you're doing is any reflection on your morals. It won't change my answer, but I'm curious now, do you have feelings for him or is it purely physical?" Piper had never engaged in girl talk before, but she assumed that was what one would call this. She was surprised to realize she actually didn't mind it. It was nice to be here with someone her own age and talk about things other than her father.

"For a while I wasn't sure. He's so different than anyone I've ever been with. He comes off as a little pretentious and arrogant, but then you get to know him and you see he isn't like that at all. The sex is incredible. No, it's more than that—it is life changing. I'm pretty sure if Michael and I don't work out I'll have to go on a quest for the rest of my life looking for something as satisfying. The man is like a machine. He never gets tired of finding ways to drive me crazy. I feel like I've enrolled in a Kama Sutra class."

Piper didn't make eye contact through this part of the conversation. This level of girl talk clearly took more practice. She wasn't quite ready to discuss Michael's sexual expertise. She wanted to be able to look him in the eye next time she saw him, not in the crotch. If Jules started talking anatomy or size she'd need to cut her off there.

Luckily, Jules took it a different direction. "I think what I'm struggling with is maybe I don't know what it's supposed to feel like anymore to be in love. Bobby was my first love, but now looking back, it was so familiar and comfortable that I feel like we loved each other the way you'd love family.

"Then I dated a few guys after him, mostly local guys who just kind of sputtered along in life, going from work to home to a fridge full of beer and sports on television, then back to work the next day. Scott...well he was a whole other story. I'm afraid I won't know what love is when I find it. Despite how good I feel when I'm with Michael, maybe there's more out there for me. How do you feel when you're with Bobby?" Jules had begun filling the spaces between her toes with cotton as she readied them for polish. She hardly looked up as she spoke, but Piper could hear the weariness in her voice. She'd clearly been giving this all a lot of thought.

"When I found Bobby I felt like I'd been driving alone for days and he came along and took the wheel. Instead of that scaring me like it has in the past, I felt so relieved, so grateful. I'm not sure, but I think love is different for everyone. I think it's about finding the person who shows up and fills in whatever holes you have, and you do the same for him. He doesn't exploit your insecurities; he calms them. He patches you up and dusts you off, and the whole time he's doing that he never takes his eyes off you. When you're with him are you more yourself than you are without him?" Putting into words what finding Bobby had done for her struck Piper in the heart. She felt a warm pang of emotion as she talked about finding the man who helped her find herself.

Jules could see the impact on Piper's face, and even as she contemplated her own situation she found joy in what Bobby and Piper had found in each other. "If I put my pride aside, and stop worrying he may not feel the same way, then yes I want something more with him. I know I'm dramatic and impatient. I can be rash and I hold grudges for an unhealthy length of time. I went out and married that idiot Scott just to spite Bobby's career choice. But when I'm with Michael, I take an extra breath before I speak. I don't want to be melodramatic and reckless with my words. I watch him, the way he carries himself. I listen to him, hear how intelligent he is, and it makes me proud. He's not even really mine to be proud of, but that's how I feel. The way people look at him, the way they respect him—it makes me want to be a better person myself."

"That's a pretty good start," Piper said, impressed by the amount of thought Jules had given the situation.

"But I couldn't tell you what he'd need from me. He has everything. Well, there is one thing I'm giving him, but I suppose he could get that a lot of different places."

"I'm sure it's more than that for him. I think the womanizing thing is just an act." Piper had spent enough time watching Michael and Jules together to see that he felt something, even if he wasn't shouting it from the mountaintops.

Jules blew out a loud sigh and dropped her head back. "There never seems like a good time to bring it up. What if he doesn't want the same thing as me? Then what? It's not like we can just not see each other. Things are so complicated right now, maybe I should keep my mouth shut until all this blows over, and then we can talk about it when he doesn't feel obligated to be with me."

Piper looked down at her nails and realized she had done a terrible job. She had hoped painting them would be some kind of innate girl skill that would just exist within her. This was not the case. She reached for the cotton balls and polish remover and started to wipe it away. "I wouldn't wait." Piper shrugged. Maybe she was still on some kind of enthusiastic high caused by the long awaited night she spent with Bobby yesterday.

Everything seemed like it had a simple answer when you'd spent hours clawing at the sheets and shuddering with pleasure. *Yes, confront that complicated issue. Of course you should ask for a raise. Confess your love? Absolutely.* No one should be able to give advice after a night like that. Apparently for a pessimist like Piper, orgasms equated to rose-colored glasses.

"Life is short, Jules. If Michael makes you feel something special, then tell him. Just be honest. I think the sooner the better. He's a very even-keeled guy, I'm sure he'll appreciate your leveling with him."

Jules, contemplating Piper's advice, looked down and caught a glimpse of her hands. "What did you do to yourself?" Jules hollered, referring to the red smears running down Piper's fingers. "That's not how you put nail polish on, and it's not how you take it off, either. Didn't your mom ever show you how to do this?" The moment the words passed her lips Jules knew she had screwed up. "I'm sorry," she whispered sheepishly.

"Don't be sorry," Piper replied. "Just get over here and take this junk off me. It's burning like hell, and I'm pretty sure I'm flammable at this point."

Jules hopped off her bed and walked on her heels to keep her freshly polished toes from touching the carpet. She wasn't sure if Piper had meant it to be, but Jules took the quick forgiveness of her stupidity as a sign that Piper didn't mind talking about her past. Jules was curious. She wanted to know what Piper had lived through, what brought her to this point in her life.

"What was it like?" Jules asked, as she took the cotton and nail polish remover from Piper and began fixing the damage on her hands. "Growing up, what was it like for you?"

Piper looked at her messy hands and then slowly back at Jules. She had never had anyone to talk to about her past before she came to Edenville. Then when she'd found people interested, she hadn't been allowed to. Now there was nothing stopping her except her own self-consciousness of how the truth might change the way someone looked at her. But she needed to trust, and Jules had never given her reason not to.

"It was bad." A simple statement, but it was the truth. "I guess I didn't know how bad it was until I was older and I realized other people didn't live the way we did. My parents were both drug addicts. They were very violent, though in different ways. They were neglectful to the point that there were times I'm amazed I didn't die of malnutrition or an untreated illness. I've tried to convince myself a few times that my mom did the best she could, but then I look at your mom and I realize she had a long way to go. I didn't learn anything that's of any use in the real world. I can ration food, I can hide in small spaces for long periods of time, and I can take a hell of a punch. But I can't paint my nails. I can't cook a meal. I can't for the life of me figure out how to fold a fitted sheet."

Jules smirked. "No one knows how to do that. My mother even rolls them up into a ball and crams them in the linen closet, so don't feel too bad about that one." Jules focused only on Piper's disastrous fingernails, not wanting to make her uncomfortable by showing sadness for her. "Did you love your parents?"

That was a question Piper had never been asked before. It wasn't even something she'd asked herself. There were so many layers to it, so much scar tissue built on that query. She was glad Jules had asked, because now she was curious about the answer, too.

"Did I ever love my parents? I'm not sure. I think when you're beaten down and then given small pieces of hope, even in the form of a fast food cheeseburger, you tend to blur the line of dependence and love. I don't have a specific memory of loving either of my parents, but there were days I didn't hate them. There were days they provided something I was so desperate for, like food or even peace and quiet, that I was grateful to them. My father had moments of kindness, and times when it felt like he might have loved me, but once I found out about his crimes that all became very tainted. I was given a file of all the murders he had been accused of committing, and the dates often lined up with moments of calm in our lives.

"Apparently whatever had built up in him would spill over in the form of murder. Then it would release the pressure, and he'd be normal for a little while. But, inevitably, he'd lose control again. It makes me sick now to think how happy I would be for those short periods of time, when in reality someone had just violently lost a daughter, a sister, a friend. Did I love my parents? No," Piper concluded, "not even in that obedient way that tells you that you're supposed to. It makes me sad to admit it, but it isn't worth lying about. I can't change it now. What was more frightening to me was the thought of never loving anyone, or no one ever loving me. Now that I don't have to worry about that any more, it's a little easier to cope with the rest of it." Piper looked down at her hands, amazed that Jules was able to get every last hint of the red polish off her.

"Do you think it was your father who attacked that girl on campus? In your heart, do you feel like he's here?" Jules imagined that kind of evil would carry with it a force that could be felt by anyone who had experienced it. Piper knew it was a perk found only in the movies. There was no homing device to let her know when danger was near. She had no spidey-sense.

"I really can't say. My gut tells me, no, he isn't here in Edenville. Nothing about that crime felt like my father had committed it. Maybe I'm just trying to be optimistic, but I don't think it's him."

"I'm sorry you went through that. I can't imagine what it must have felt like, and I'm really in awe of how you came through it. Thanks for listening to my boring, pedestrian relationship worries and not looking at me like I'm some self-absorbed brat. I know this stuff with Michael and me isn't important compared to what you're dealing with." Jules was embarrassed now for even bringing up her silly issues.

"Jules, my problems have become all our problems. We're in this together. I'm glad you talked to me about what's going on with you and Michael. I care so much about you both, and, no matter what, I want to see you happy. I think you should talk to him." Jules threw her arms around Piper and pulled her in for a hug. None of this was easy, but it felt a little less hopeless when she had someone to talk to.

"Thank you so much." Jules released her from the tight bear hug and ran her fingers through Piper's thick hair. "Do you know how to put rollers in?" she asked with an excited grin. "I could teach you." Jules had found the perfect student for her fashion and beauty techniques.

"Aren't those for, like, a perm?" Piper asked, not able to

keep the endless line of styling products straight. Jules shook her head and furrowed her brows looking at Piper's nails again.

"Maybe we should start small, I'll get the curling iron and the hairspray." She scurried to the bathroom, but turned back toward Piper with a laugh. "Maybe I should bring the aloe and Band-Aids, too."

Chapter Five

THERE WERE A few things Piper could always count on. If she were at Betty's house she'd be fed. If she were with Michael she'd be teased. If she spent the day with Jules there would be some kind of makeover. And Bobby, he was just unwaveringly available and reliable. He *always* answered his phone, even if it was just to say he was busy and would call back. But for the last five hours Piper had been getting his voicemail. They had spent another amazing night at his place—take-out, wine, and hours of passion that had her legs buckling from exhaustion this morning. He'd brought her to levels of ecstasy she'd never imagined possible. When she was convinced her body could take no more, he'd found a way to show her it could. Now her mind, in between moments of worry, flashed the scenes of their night together. She'd opened her heart and given her body over to him with a trust she'd never dabbled in before. It was as terrifying as it was satisfying.

Bobby had left for duty that morning and kissed her lips softly before dropping her at Michael's office. She was now driving Michael crazy with her nervous fidgeting.

"Do you think I should call the precinct?" Piper asked for the third time.

"I'm not going to change my answer no matter how many times you ask. No, you shouldn't call the precinct. Bobby's working, he's probably tied up with something, and he'll call you when he can. Or maybe he dropped his phone in the toilet. I did that two months ago, I missed plenty of calls. Just relax." Piper thought if she were ever in charge of the world she'd make it against the law to direct those two words at a woman. Saying, "just relax" would warrant a bloody beating for any man dumb enough to utter the phrase.

Michael smiled as he handed Piper a blank notebook and pen. "When clients come in with their kids who can't sit still I always give them these. Why don't you draw me something nice?"

"I can write up your will for you, you're about to need one," Piper grumbled back at him. Suddenly, Michael's receptionist, Irene, a small masculine looking woman with an outdated hairstyle, knocked lightly on the door and stepped in. Piper always laughed a little inside when she saw her. She recalled how Michael had bragged to her early on in their friendship how he had slept his way through many receptionists who promptly quit upon their break-ups. He'd boasted that women had a difficult time working for him and not *wanting more.* Through some friendly conversations with Irene, Piper found out that there had been no other receptionists. Irene had worked at the firm for nearly five years before Michael had started there, and she'd been the only one he'd ever worked with. There was nothing like a man and his ego, using fake conquests to trump up his status. It was laughable, especially when Irene would come by, because she clearly had no problem keeping her hands off Michael.

"Mr. Cooper," Irene said evenly, "Officer Wright is here to see you. He has some other folks with him. He says it's urgent."

Michael couldn't hold his steady poker face. He looked at Piper, letting her know he had no idea what this was all about. "Send them in," he said, sounding hesitant.

At the sight of the group filing into Michael's office, Piper's heart sank. Her two worlds had just collided, and more than that, the one person she trusted more than anyone had seemingly betrayed her. Every stabbing pain she'd buried away came blasting back. Her mind went from too full, to instantly empty, dumping out like a bucket of water. Bobby was the first to enter the office, and directly behind him was Agent Lydia Carlson, a dark-haired, dark-skinned woman with piercing caramel-colored eyes. She kept her hair short and swept to the side, her clothes pristine and pressed, and her full lips shining with gloss. She reminded Piper of a tiger, fierce eyes and intense jaw, always looking like she was about to growl. She could put large gold hoop earrings on and as much black mascara as she'd like, but as far as Piper was concerned, underneath it all was a primal animal hunting its prey.

Piper met Bobby's eyes for only a second and then looked away, knowing the tears would come if she kept her gaze on him. She battled back the urge to vomit, her stomach doing somersaults. Instead she looked back at Michael and lifted her chin in angry defiance, and in that instant it all made sense to him.

Bobby cleared his throat. "Michael, this is Special Agent Carlson. She's the head of the task force to catch the Railway Killer. This is Agent Fuentes," he continued, pointing to the tall Hispanic man who extended his hand to greet Michael, "the head of the criminal profiling unit."

"Isabella," Special Agent Carlson began curtly, "I'm glad to see you are doing well. Better than the two girls who were recently attacked here in Edenville, for certain. Had you not heard the news?" Carlson spoke condescension as if it were a second language she had learned. Yes, Piper thought to herself, Carlson was bilingual in "bitch."

Before Piper could retort, Bobby cut in. "As we talked about earlier, Special Agent Carlson, there was no way for her to know if the cases were linked to her father. There are quite a few inconsistencies between past attacks and the ones that have occurred here in Edenville." Piper was piecing together the puzzle now. There had been a second attack this morning. And now Bobby's overwhelming instincts to protect the public had undermined his loyalty to her. He had gone to his captain with the information he had, and the FBI was called in. Then Agent Carlson flew in on her broomstick.

"My name is Piper," she said, with her back still to them. Michael's face was red, either with discomfort or anger; Piper couldn't distinguish which.

"Not anymore it isn't," Special Agent Carlson said tersely. Turning her attention to Bobby, she opened her large notepad and pulled a pen from her breast pocket. "If what you told me on the phone was correct, and her father has found her, then the identity of Piper Anderson no longer exists. Isabella will be entered back into witness protection. She'll be given a new identity and moved immediately."

The room was spinning now as Piper tried to digest Special Agent Carlson's words. "I'm not going anywhere. I have a life here. He isn't going to take that from me."

"He isn't here to spoil your fun or wreck your social life," Carlson shot back. "There are things here that you don't understand."

"So then explain them to me," Piper snapped.

"Fine," Carlson huffed back. "You know that your father is a serial killer. He killed twenty-three women, one of which was your mother. He made an attempt on your life, but you survived. You were the only one of his victims to do so. Because there was a lag in time when you didn't identify him after your attack, another girl was murdered—Delanie Morrison, who he thought was his twenty-fourth victim."

Special Agent Carlson was trying to allude to the fact that if Piper had been more forthcoming with the information about her father immediately after her own attack, then perhaps they could have caught him in time. Perhaps Delanie would still be alive. Piper didn't need the reminder, though, because that weight sat next to her every day like a melancholy ghost. It was heavy on her heart at all times. Piper hadn't wanted to believe she was the product of a serial killer. She had already been through so much.

So two years ago when Special Agent Carlson questioned her about her attack, and Piper became aware of her father's other crimes, she stayed silent. Weeks later, Delanie Morrison was dead with the number twenty-four carved into her leg. Her femoral artery was severed with the same railroad spike that had been driven into Piper's leg. As Special Agent Carlson retold this memory, Bobby saw the same sadness and guilt creep across Piper's face that had on the day she had finally told him about her past. He'd had just about enough of this.

"Easy," Bobby cut in, looking sternly at Carlson. "You're getting off track. Piper's a victim here. It's your job to find the murderer, not hers." The woman seemed to lack any empathy. Bobby understood the seriousness of the situation, but treating Piper like a child wasn't going to move the case forward.

"Anyway," Special Agent Carlson continued, letting the word draw out with far more attitude than Bobby thought necessary, "after we did *finally* identify him, it was leaked to the press that there was a break in the case and that one of his victims, Isabella, had survived. Now out of the blue two girls are attacked here in this Podunk town where you've been relocated. The Criminal Profiling Unit has spent years on your father's case. With the events of the week here in Edenville they've come up with an assessment. Your father is compulsive. Whatever mechanism in his brain makes him a serial killer also makes him a slave to his own routine. He can't deviate from his compulsions. He hasn't murdered anyone in over two years. We believe when your father found out you were still alive, his world was turned upside down. That number he carved in your leg means something to him, something we can't even begin to understand. We believe he isn't able to kill anyone else until he finishes what he started with you. He's probably been hunting you this whole time, and now he's found you. You are the only thing standing in the way of his ability to keep killing. You're the itch he needs to scratch."

Carlson cleared her throat and went on speaking, frustration filling her voice as Piper still refused to turn in her chair and make eye contact. "*Isabella*, I know this is difficult. Relocation often is, but this is your only option. Your father will stop at nothing to kill you. He needs you dead in order to feed that beast inside him. I'm going to draw up the papers and give you a chance to say goodbye." She put her pen back into her pocket. Piper had no words. She looked helplessly at Michael who, up until now, seemed bewildered by the entourage that had just plowed its way into his office.

Finally he shook his head as if he was breaking free of a fog, and found his words. "Special Agent Carlson," he started, deepening his voice a little for effect, "I can understand your urgency and concern here. You have been working this case for quite a while and haven't been successful in apprehending a very dangerous man. That must be discouraging." *And embarrassing*, Michael thought to himself. "I think, however, you might be jumping the gun here. Has the medical examiner determined if the cases are linked? Have any eyewitnesses come forward? It seems like there are still many unanswered questions. Perhaps prior to initiating a very serious process like witness protection, we should let some of this play out. Don't you agree?"

Michael wasn't actually sure how he felt about the whole situation. If he were looking at this merely as a prosecutor he'd be driving Piper to the airport right now, making sure his witness was safe. But knowing Piper the way he did, he understood routine relocation was not the answer. When her big doe eyes glassed over with the hint of tears, her bristly exterior cracked, and he wanted to throw himself in front of her like a human shield. It was clear she needed as much emotional protection as she did physical.

"Who the hell are you?" Agent Carlson barked. "The only reason we're in your office right now is because this is where we knew we would find Isabella. Besides that, I can't see how this has anything to do with you."

"First, I think for the sake of ease, it would be best if you called this young lady by the name she prefers. It seems as though she does not want to be called by the name she gave up when she entered witness protection. I'm sure an agent with all your years of experience can understand the importance of respecting the wishes of a victim. Second, my name is Michael Cooper. I'm apparently the person who's going to *encourage* you, and I leave that word open to interpretation, to do your job thoroughly and complete the investigation before taking such drastic measures. Now, when should we expect the medical examiner's report regarding the wounds on the girls' legs? Have the Internet fan pages dedicated to the Railway Killer been cross-referenced with any IP addresses in or around Edenville? Has surveillance footage at all gas stations and ATM machines within a two mile radius been checked for suspicious activity around the time of the attacks?" Piper felt her back straighten slightly. She had wanted Bobby to stand by her on this. Her heart was broken that he hadn't, but at least she wasn't completely alone.

Carlson wasn't one to be easily intimidated. She stepped in front of Piper, who had not even spared her a glance up until this point. Now Piper met her icy gaze straight on. "Are you saying you don't want the protection being offered to you, *Piper*? If you choose to waive that, we cannot ensure your safety or the safety of any of the people you care about. Your father will exploit every relationship you have in order to get to you. If you do not take our offer of witness protection, then you are on your own. The task force has scaled back significantly over the last couple years since your father has gone dormant. We don't have the means to offer you anything in the way of security."

"I can protect her. I can protect all of them," Bobby insisted, wishing to draw Carlson's attention away from Piper the way one might throw a rock at a bear to stop it from attacking someone. And just like that scenario, once the bear turns your way, you had better be ready for an attack of your own.

"Oh yes," Carlson sneered, "the rookie cop who keeps stepping in piles of shit. Your reputation precedes you, Office Wright. Have you learned the Miranda Rights yet?" And there it was. The stabbing pains of regret filled Bobby. He had done what he thought was right, the only option he felt he had, and now he was faced with the fact that he had brought in the one person Piper needed the least. The cold, calloused agent who had kicked her when she was down and was lining up to do it again. This woman had manipulated and mentally destroyed Piper by leveraging Delanie's death, and he'd practically rolled out the red carpet for her to do it again.

"I'll be in touch," Carlson continued as she pulled open the door. "With any luck you learned from your mistake last time and will do the right thing before someone else gets killed." She waved for Agent Fuentes to come with her but ignored Bobby all together. He had planned to stay for a while to talk to Piper anyway.

"Piper," Bobby said, crouching down in front of where she still sat stiffly in her chair. "You have to understand why I did this. There was another attack this morning. I have an obligation to this community."

"Get the hell out of here." Piper gulped back her tears, her rage, and her pain. "You're not going to convince me you did the right thing here. We're not going to agree on this. Just go do your job since that seems to be the most important thing to you right now." When he opened his mouth to speak again she cut in, "Go."

Bobby looked over at Michael, hoping for an ally, thinking he might chime in and convince Piper there was no other choice. But Michael stayed silent. Bobby had told himself all morning, no matter how badly Piper took the news that he had contacted the FBI, he wouldn't waver in his belief that he had done the right thing. He had all but convinced himself, no matter how hurt she looked, no matter how broken, he'd done the right thing. He promised himself he'd remember the oath he took when he became a police officer and it would carry him past the doubt in his mind. Promise broken. He left the room quietly, his head hanging.

Michael stood for another minute in disbelief of what had just transpired in the quick but impactful five minutes. When he saw Piper looking like she'd slipped into a state of shock he realized if his head was spinning, Piper's must be ready to pop. He crossed his office and sat in the chair next to her, pulling it a little closer. She leaned forward, bracing her elbows on her knees and cradled her head in her hands as she groaned.

He rubbed her back in a soothing circular motion and ached when her tears started to fall. He wrestled with himself: what to say, how to comfort? Then, before he could convince himself it was too soon, he said, "I guess you can look on the bright side." He peeked down at her wet eyes as she turned her head slightly to see what bright side he could possibly be talking about. "At least he didn't drop his phone in the toilet."

She sat up quickly and he assumed it was to be in a better position to yell at him. He braced himself for a punch in the shoulder or a slap on the face. It wouldn't be his first, and if it made her feel better to hit him, then he'd be willing to take a punch. Instead she wrinkled her brows and had an odd crooked, almost confused smile. "Oh please, a straight and narrow guy like Bobby? He'd have a back-up memory card and a spare phone ready to go."

Chapter Six

"I STILL CAN'T believe he did that. He's lucky it was a loaf of bread and not a brick I threw at him," Jules said, still angry every time she thought about Bobby's betrayal. It had been two days and her anger hadn't lessened a bit, so she could only imagine how Piper felt.

"Just be glad you weren't there when it happened," Michael said, running his hands through his hair in that mindless but sexy way he always did. "Bobby stormed into my office with some egomaniac special agent and completely blindsided Piper. It was so uncomfortable. He should have handled it differently," Michael remarked, recalling the disastrous afternoon.

"He shouldn't have called the FBI at all. He knew they would try to get her to move away. Does he really want that to happen?" Jules couldn't understand why Bobby would, once again, let his job come between him and the person he supposedly loved.

"I actually think he did the right thing," Michael admitted. "I just don't agree with how he did it. He should have let Piper know what to expect, given her the courtesy of a heads-up. And he should have put that overbearing special agent in her place before she ever saw Piper. I know he was trying to do the right thing, but man, he really blew it."

"Where is Piper now? I know Bobby is at the house with Ma, who has been tearing him a new one for days," Jules said, feeling lucky she wasn't there to catch any of the wrath.

"I put her up in a cabin that belongs to a client of mine. It's out by the river. She said she needed some space. I've never seen her look so hurt." Michael hesitated, thinking again of the uncontrollable sobs coming from Piper after Bobby had left his office. His attempts at humor hadn't worked as well as he had hoped. Inevitably the little smile she had plastered on her face had faded and the tears had come. "The place has a very advanced security system and I called in a favor so she could borrow Bruno."

"Who's Bruno?" asked Jules. She couldn't help picturing a hulking bodyguard standing vigil at the door of the cabin.

"He's a police dog, or he's going to be. My buddy trains them. Bruno is just about to graduate from the training program, and he'll be good protection and good company. She'll need it. Every time I talk to her on the phone she seems okay, but honestly I think she's in pretty rough shape. They're in love though, they'll figure it out."

At the mention of love, Jules bit at her bottom lip as she fought with herself about how to broach her conversation with Michael. They'd stopped by La Bella Luna to pick up some takeout for lunch. They'd planned to spend the afternoon eating, drinking wine, and making love. She knew whatever she said, however she said it, almost didn't matter. It would be what he said in response that would determine how the rest of the evening went.

"Michael, we need to talk," Jules finally blurted, the words bursting out of her like water raging down a river. Michael had heard this short but meaningful phrase dozens of times in his adult life. In his experience, women were not comfortable with casual sex for more than a month or so. They talked a good game, but when it came down to it, inevitably they all sat in front of him with the we-need-to-talk look in their eyes.

He'd had a feeling it would be coming with Jules, too, but he'd hoped it wouldn't. Nothing good ever came of it. This conversation was one he had mastered. Guilt, deflect, procrastinate, they leave—start over. That wasn't what he wanted with Jules, but old habits die hard.

"Sure, we can talk about anything," he replied calmly. Step one: even if you know what's coming don't act annoyed. That instantly made you look like the bad guy.

"Maybe this isn't the right time to talk about this. Things are so complicated, but it's really weighing on my mind. I know we're very different people. I'm a Catholic. I try to live my life a certain way. You play more by your own rules. I feel like we need to talk about where all this is going. I'm not sure I'm comfortable with just having a physical relationship. It's not who I am. I'm not judging you or anything, I just can't keep going this way."

Michael felt hurt as he took in her words. Maybe he wasn't sitting in church every Sunday, or any Sunday, but he certainly wasn't basking in the warmth of the devil's fire either. She was making his part much easier to execute now. Step two: turn the conversation around. Forget what she's asking; make her feel like she never should have asked in the first place. He knew it was manipulative and very wrong, but this was just how it went with him and women. Even if being with Jules felt different, even if he could see himself with her for the long haul, this was how he dealt with the question of labeling a relationship.

"I hear what you're saying. You don't want to have some casual fling, I can understand that. If you aren't comfortable, I'd never want to pressure you. Let's just keep things from getting physical. We're adults, I think we can both handle that." Michael laid that line down like someone showing a winning hand at poker.

"That isn't what I'm saying at all. I love what we're doing physically, I've never had anything so fulfilling in my life. I don't want it to stop. I'm sorry that I'm not being clear, I'm having a hard time saying what I mean." Jules bit again at her lip, and Michael could see her eyes growing glassy with tears. No, he thought to himself, please do not cry. Normally he could ignore the tears of a woman, but Jules was different. He hadn't wanted to admit it, but she'd managed to worm her way through deeper layers of his heart than anyone before.

"Well, that's the thing, Jules, if you don't know what you're trying to say, how can I be expected to understand it?" He'd used this line multiple times in court. It was very effective at unsettling a witness during cross-examination and seemed to have the same effect on Jules. Her mouth was now closed tightly as she physically tried not to speak until she could feel confident in her words. But Michael knew she wouldn't, he was making sure of that. He was cutting her off, making her uneasy. He was bullying her right out of asking him how he felt about her. He wasn't ready to acknowledge any feelings for her, so instead of doing the adult thing, he attacked. And now, he thought to himself, the final blow, "Jules, you were right when you started this conversation. It isn't the right time. None of this should be about us right now. Not until Piper is out of danger.

"I know it's hard for someone like you to understand, but sometimes it's not about you. You have to put your own feelings aside. I guess that just comes with maturity." In a brief couple of sentences he had exploited every one of her insecurities. She knew she could be slightly dramatic and selfish, but now, as Michael spun the words smoothly, Jules realized this is how he saw her, and it crushed her. He had done it.

"I've been trying really hard," Jules stuttered. "I know that I can be a little over the top sometimes, but I thought you would have noticed that I've been working on that." A few warm tears rolled down her cheek and her lip quivered.

Damn it, Michael thought to himself. Why did he have to be so good at controlling a situation that he could have a perfectly amazing woman feeling like dirt? He didn't want her to be hurt. She had every right to be curious about how he felt about her, every right to want more from him. The truth was he was utterly captivated by her. And because of that, he was afraid, terrified. But instead of facing his feelings like a man, he cut her down. The words he wanted to say were, *I have noticed. You have been such a wonderful friend to Piper and such a big part of making everything work right now.* But, like the fool that he was, all he could muster was, "It's good to try I guess, but it's more about results."

With that Jules stood. "I guess you're right. I shouldn't have brought this up today. I'm really sorry for being so silly." She wiped the tears from her eyes and grabbed her coat from the hook by the door. "I need to get a little air; I'll be back in a few minutes."

"I don't think that's a great idea. You shouldn't be wandering around down there. It's not safe." Michael was concerned about the danger but, more so, about watching her leave wounded, especially as he was the one inflicting the pain.

"It's the middle of the day, I'll just be a minute," Jules called as she closed the door behind her.

Chapter Seven

DARK. THAT'S ALL Piper could feel. Her insides felt shadowy and twisted. She hadn't anticipated the difference between being betrayed by people you always knew would hurt you versus people you think never would. Piper likened it to floating in a murky swamp all her life, feeling cold, dirty, and utterly alone. Then a boat came along, warm, welcoming, and safe. But all of a sudden her boat was capsized by betrayal. The water is much colder, the darkness and loneliness more intense, the pain more acute. She never knew what she was missing when she was born into the swamp, but damn the people who pulled her out only to throw her back in. They are the most dangerous of all. That's how she saw Bobby's call to the FBI— as pure betrayal.

Now here she was perched in a cabin Michael had arranged for her. She was exactly where she was meant to be. Her soul felt woven into the knotted weathered wood. She was one with the ticking clock and humming florescent light. There was nothing personal in this house. No family pictures, no height chart carved in the threshold of a doorway measuring the sprouting children that might have lived here. This place was void of life, past or present, and that was exactly how she felt. She had barely paid attention to its exterior, but vaguely remembered it was small, nondescript, and tucked away among the sturdy oaks and towering pines that were so characteristic of North Carolina. This was the perfect retreat for her.

In the two days she had spent in the cabin, Piper hadn't turned on a single light. She didn't even know where the switches were, and she didn't care. When night fell, she sat perfectly still, dozing occasionally, but mostly just staring, fixing her gaze on a random picture or decoration in the unfamiliar house. She could hear the moving water of the Eno River that cut through the clearing just twenty feet behind the house. She had perched herself in the living room, eaten only enough to quiet her stomach, and let the sadness blanket her.

She couldn't believe the contrast she felt between the comforting quiet of Betty's porch and the suffocating silence of this place. But this was a tried and true method for easing her pain. Sit still. Sit perfectly still, don't make a single ripple in the world. Contain yourself to the smallest space, and fight the voice in your head, beat it back. Keep it quiet. Keep still.

Maybe people diagnose this as depression, but she didn't want the terms, the medicine, or the therapy. This ache was familiar to her; part of her didn't want it to heal. Piper returned to this darkness the way some people returned to a place they had visited as a child, wanting to feel the comfort of a friendly hug. This was where her childhood memories resided; this was the feeling most familiar to her.

The only force that kept pulling her out of her own black hole of sorrow was the wet nose of Bruno. He would occasionally nudge her arm and lay his heavy head on her lap. Michael had insisted she take the two-year-old German Shepherd with her to the cabin. He implied it was for her protection, but she assumed he also wanted Bruno to keep her company. As much as she hated to admit it, Bruno was pretty decent company. He wasn't overly excitable; he took his lead from her. When she sat motionless, he curled beside her feet and his body rose and fell with steady breaths, just as hers did. When she stood to get a drink or something to eat, he stood, followed, and watched her every move.

There were only two rules in caring for Bruno. Rule one: don't take any cocaine in front of him, as this would initiate his training as a police dog. Piper knew this "rule" was an attempt at humor on Michael's part. But the second rule he clearly meant. He had told her that under no circumstance was Bruno to eat anything except his special food. No treats, no table food. As part of the positive-reinforcement-training schedule utilized by the K-9 program, the dogs are given treats after they appropriately perform desired tasks. Giving them treats while they are not "on the job" can confuse the dogs and undermine their training. Michael reiterated that Bruno was still in school, so he was very impressionable, and therefore Piper needed to stick with his feeding and exercise routines. The thought of that conversation made Piper grin as she handed Bruno another potato chip. She patted his head lightly as he licked at his chops for more.

So far he had taken a liking to pickles, lunchmeat, and bread in addition to the chips. Piper had such a lack of appetite it seemed a waste to throw out a sandwich after just two bites. She loved the way Bruno's eyes lit every time he heard the crinkling of a food wrapper. His ears would perk up, and he would move closer to her, politely begging. She wasn't sure what it was about defying the clearly spelled out rule that made her slightly happy in the face of such sadness, but when that sweet-faced dog got a mouthful of bologna it eased her pain a little. Why shouldn't Bruno taste the best parts of life? Why should he be forced to eat the same meal every day, to sniff some smelly shirt and track a criminal through thick brush and rocky terrain. He didn't seem like he really even wanted to be that kind of dog. He loved lying around, cuddling on the couch, and eating junk food. And Piper liked having him here. He didn't make any promises he couldn't keep, he didn't profess any deep feelings, he just existed next to her, kept her warm, and, most importantly, made her feel safe.

His hearing was incredible. Every unusual noise had him sitting at attention, just as he had learned in his training. Piper had been given the code phrase, "Bruno, defend." When accompanied by a snap of the finger, this command would send him into a fierce growl with exposed teeth that would frighten anyone. But if it didn't frighten them, she had been assured he had the strength and ability to back up that growl. His primary job, however, was tracking. The trainer had told her and

Michael the day they picked Bruno up that he had never met a dog with a keener nose. He really didn't have all the other skills of a police dog perfectly mastered—he had a tendency to be distracted and bordered on lazy—but that nose, it was something special.

Piper offered him another handful of chips and tried to work up the energy to walk over to the back door and let Bruno out for some fresh air. The trainer had insisted that it was crucial for the dog to go out for at least two runs a day, consisting of at least two miles each. At the time, Piper eagerly agreed to this condition, though she had no intention of fulfilling her end of the bargain.

So far, the dog hadn't walked more than ten feet from the back door to do his business before lazily slinking back into the house to plop himself down next to her. Bruno's head shot up suddenly, causing Piper to pull her hand back and cover her heart as it jumped with fear. He quickly dismounted the couch, which he was not allowed to lie on according to the trainer, and headed for the front door. Someone was coming. Piper crept behind him and peeked out of the lacy curtain on the front door as she nervously flipped open the cover to the alarm system. She let her finger hover over the panic button. Michael had assured her that it was linked directly to the police and the owner had paid buckets of money to make sure it would result in immediate response. She hadn't asked who the client was or what their need for such a system would be, she was just glad to have it.

Bruno let out a low growl as a rusted blue car pulled up the driveway. Like a weight being lifted off her chest, Piper huffed loudly and gave the command, "Bruno, stand down" and snapped her fingers. Bruno immediately lowered his ears and sat obediently by her feet. As Betty stepped with purpose out of her car, Piper readied herself for an emotional encounter. She thought for a moment. Maybe she'd let Bruno's loud bark scare Betty away. But who was she kidding? This dog, *any* dog, would be no match for a woman like Betty. Piper would have to let her in and face reality.

Betty rapped softly on the glass, and Piper pulled the door open without a word. Betty was better at finding words, at knowing what to say. It was easier to be silent and wait to hear what she'd come up with.

"Oh sweetheart," Betty's arms were stretched wide and her face was pulled down with emotion. Piper stepped backward, evaded Betty's offer of a hug and crossed her arms over her own stomach instead. Her lesson had been learned, if you let yourself feel the joy that comes from being hugged by someone who loves you, then you have to prepare yourself for the hole it leaves when it's no longer an option. But if you avoid the warmth of the hug, then the cold you live in all the time doesn't feel quite so cold. Betty didn't need to hear those words to interpret Piper's behavior. Her first instinct was to barge in and lecture Piper on the idiocy of protecting your heart. Of how isolating herself was not the solution. That's the speech she'd have given to almost anyone in her life, but Piper was different. There was no blaming her for what she'd been through, and just the fact that she woke up every day and found a way to put one foot in front of the other was a testament to her strength. No, Betty thought, this child doesn't need harsh words today.

"I'm so sorry how things have happened, Piper. I wish I could take all this away from you. This burden is far too heavy for one person to carry alone. Will you let me come in and try to carry some of it with you?"

Piper swallowed hard as she thought to herself, *Damn you Betty, why couldn't you come in here with verbal guns blazing and try to snap me out of this with some no-nonsense sermon about feeling bad for myself. Then at least I could blame you for being overbearing and insensitive. But no, here you are trying to carry my burden.* "Come on in," Piper said finally as she gave up arguing with herself.

Betty, fearing the invitation might be fleeting, stepped in swiftly. "This place seems nice, have you been sleeping okay? I brought you some groceries and some moonshine. I figured if you weren't up for eating at least we could get boiled as an owl together." Betty gestured down to the old jelly jar filled with the potent concoction.

"I'm doing fine. I really just want to be alone. I know that's hard to understand. I'm sure you like to be surrounded by people when you are going through something tough, but I do better by myself. I appreciate your coming, but really, I don't want you to get in the middle of any of this. I'm not sure Bobby and I will ever get this right, and I know he's like a son to you." Piper felt weary as she spoke, the hours of not moving and hardly eating had caught up with her now that she was forced to be upright and actually use her brain.

"I'm not in the middle of anything, I can promise you that. I'm firmly planted on your side of the fence on this one. That boy was flat-out wrong. He owed you a warning. Hell I'm not even sure calling those uptight know-it-alls at the FBI was the right thing at all. He handled it in a very cowardly way as far as I'm concerned, and he's hiding behind the job again. I told him if he keeps putting his career first, the only thing he's ever going to wake up next to is that badge. Ain't no one going to keep sitting second fiddle to his ideals. Don't get me wrong, I want you safe, and I feel terrible for those girls that have been hurt, but you deserved better than that. You've earned it from him." Betty had made her way into the kitchen as she finished speaking and pulled open the refrigerator, loading it with food she had brought. Piper was speechless for a moment.

This wasn't at all how she imagined this would go. Well, short of the food. She knew Betty would never dream of visiting empty-handed. She fought the urge to speak earnestly with Betty, but as the woman packed the refrigerator with all of Piper's favorite things, she couldn't help but cave.

"Thanks, Betty. It means a lot to me that you'd come here and that you have my back on this. I can't understand why he didn't call me first and let me know what he was doing. How could he just storm in like that and then let Agent Carlson ambush me? I felt like I was looking at a stranger instead of the man I'm in love with. It doesn't make any sense to me. It hurt so much, and he doesn't even seem to think he did anything wrong."

"I swear that Carlson lady better not cross me. I've heard all about how she treats you, and I won't stand for that. As for Bobby, he knows he screwed up, I can assure you of that. He's had an earful from me, and I know it's hitting him hard." Betty moved back toward Piper but wasn't about to attempt another hug. "Every path has its puddles— yours seems to have a few land mines, too. It don't make you any less than anyone else, it just makes what you have to do harder. Love that grows through adversity is stronger than any kind of regular love. I'm not saying to forgive him. I'm not saying to run back to him. All I'm saying is, if you do make your way through this with him, you'll have something that's been tested and survived. But either way, you've got me. I'm not going anywhere."

"Why?" Piper asked, feeling the burning come back to her stomach at the thought of Bobby. "Why are you still here? What have I ever really done to make you care about me? I'm the child of a monster. His blood runs through my veins. I'm the product of something truly evil, and even if he isn't here in Edenville, he's a part of me. Why do you keep fighting so hard to see me as something better than I am?"

"You are one mixed-up girl sometimes, Piper. I'm not fighting so I can see you differently—I'm fighting for you to see *yourself* differently. Your parents don't make you who you are. My daddy was a shamefully racist man. I'm not comparing it to what you've been through, but I wasn't the daughter of a saint that's for sure. I saw him do some purely evil things in his day. I heard him treat people like they weren't worth the air they were breathing or the space they were standing in. I swore, when I was grown, when I could do it differently, I would. And you know what, I do. I open my heart and my arms to anyone who needs them. I don't care what color skin you have or who you chose to love. If God made you then he wanted me to love you, and I'll sure as hell find a way to do it. It might not sit right with everyone at my church, it might have my daddy rolling over in his grave, but I don't answer to any of them. You don't have to be what you come from. Now, I'm not here to tell you to shake this off, because that would be silly of me. You get to hurt right now, you get to hide. I'm here to tell you the world is still out there waiting for you when you are ready. I'll still be here."

Chapter Eight

BOBBY FELT LIKE a man alone on an island. All the people who normally surrounded him with support had deserted him. Betty managed to work up a lecture every time they were together. She'd told him about the dangers of choosing anything over love and the pitfalls of misplaced priorities. Jules had flat out called him an ass and nearly took his head off with a loaf of bread she hurled in his direction. Michael, though more sympathetic than the others, seemed disappointed in his friend.

Bobby was trying hard to live by the mantra, *I had no choice.* But the longer he spent isolated from his friends, the more time that passed since he'd last heard Piper's voice or touched her silky skin, the more doubt crept in. It was like a vine infiltrating, taking over. On the flip side, the guys at work and even Agent Carlson kept slapping him on the back and telling him he'd be ready for detective in no time. His captain, the blustery narcissist, Baines, had pulled Bobby aside and given him a bottle of single malt scotch. His way of thanking him for making the whole department look good, Bobby guessed. And yet none of that mattered when the people he cared for most thought he was a jackass.

He knew Betty had gone to visit Piper that afternoon and though he wanted to ask for an update he reconsidered. He knew Betty would probably remind him that he'd given up his right to know how she was doing. Tired of the silence that had taken over Betty's house since she had gone upstairs to bed, Bobby turned on the television, looking for an escape. The nightly news was just starting, and he found himself staring at the beautiful anchorwoman as she began to speak. He watched her face, stoic and serious, staring straight into the camera.

"This is Maria Santos with WNC4 news with an exclusive, late-breaking story." That was it, Bobby thought; that was the reason for the sparkle in her eye. She was about to be the first to break a big story, and she was having a hard time containing the gloating look on her face. "The town of Edenville has been rocked lately by corruption and accusations of misconduct on multiple levels. The residents here seem divided in their belief and support of those accused. We were all shocked to hear the news about Judge Lions and his association with the late Officer Rylie. Most of us thought that would be the story of the decade here in Edenville, but I'm here to report that the drama continues. Through a source very close to the investigation, we have learned of a break in the case of the two young women assaulted on campus this week. They have confirmed a link between the attacks and the infamous Railway Killer. For those of you who aren't familiar with him, the Railway Killer is one of the most notorious serial killers in recent history, and he has been very successful at evading the law over his twenty-five year reign of terror. Our source has confirmed the presence of the FBI, more specifically, the task force created to catch the Railway Killer.

"So why is Edenville, a normally safe town, suddenly a tumultuous battleground filled with predators of all kinds? This is the question on many minds tonight as people realize the dangers lurking around them. Though we've been unable to confirm this, our source spoke at length about the one surviving victim of the Railway Killer. We're only able to speculate at this point, but it sounds as though the survivor may have settled right here in Edenville, and in the process, brought with her a kind of evil this town has never seen before. I've met with several Edenville residents tonight, and they are on edge and frustrated." Bobby watched with sweaty palms and a racing heart as the camera cut away to some previously recorded interviews.

There was his barber, Tony, standing awkwardly in front of a large microphone that Maria had shoved in his face. He stammered as he spoke into it, putting his mouth closer than it needed to be. "I think it's nuts. Why would we let someone into this town to act as bait for a killer? Whoever it is should just be on their way and take whatever messed-up history they have with them. We don't need no killers here, we already have enough junk going on as it is." As he finished speaking, the camera cut again to Maria who was looking with a forced seriousness into the camera.

"Well Tom, that's the sentiment from most of the folks I talked to tonight. They all felt the last thing this town needed was added attention. More importantly, they wanted to know why the streets weren't blanketed with police and government officials. There is a serial killer on the loose here in Edenville, yet it seems to be business as usual? We'll be back in the second half of the hour tonight to keep you informed as this story progresses. I'm hoping to have a statement from Captain Baines any moment. Until then, Tom, back to you."

Bobby slammed down the remote. If he'd been at his house instead of Betty's he likely would have launched it across the room, not caring what it might break. This was the problem with the media these days, he thought to himself. It wasn't about being right, it was about being first. Why weren't the streets littered with police trying to catch a serial killer? Because there wasn't any clear evidence that he was even here. The FBI's medical examiner and forensics team were still going over the evidence to compare the two attacks on campus. No one was confirming that the Railway Killer was in Edenville, but now there it was up on the news for everyone, including the killer, wherever he was, to see. Everything that Piper had warned him about was coming to fruition, and the knot in his stomach yanked tighter as he realized this would be one more thing to drive a wedge between them. Damn you, Maria Santos, and your ego.

His phone began to vibrate and dance its way across the coffee table. He could only imagine who it was. Piper calling to accuse him of ruining her life, Jules trying to scream some new profanity at him, or maybe it was Betty calling from the phone upstairs to tell him to get the hell out of her house. As he read the screen he realized it was worse than that.

"Agent Carlson, do you have any news?"

Chapter Nine

AFTER BETTY HAD left, Piper felt her head swirling. She sat again, motionless on the couch and thought through everything Betty had told her. As the hours ticked by she curled her legs up to her chest and rested her head on the arm of the couch. Sleep took her away like a retreating wave pulling with it a tumbling seashell.

Piper was nine years old, scared, and alone. Her parents had disappeared, and a weekend that had started as carefree and liberating for her was now terrifying. It wasn't the first time her parents had left her alone with no indication as to where they were going, no money, and no food. But as night fell on the third day without them, panic started to bleed in.

She normally loved the quiet that came with their absence. She would take whatever money she had managed to find, steal, or borrow and stock up on penny candy, junk food, and an apple or two, just to make sure she was being responsible. That food was gone now. All her money was spent. She had assumed her parents would have returned by now from whatever misguided adventure they had been on. Last time they'd spent two days running drugs into the suburbs in order to pay off a debt. Prior to that, they had taken their last hundred dollars to the casino because they were "feeling lucky." But never had they been gone this long.

Then a bang on the door, a loud thud that clearly meant business. She scurried to her room, climbed up to the top of her closet and squatted on the shelf above the door that was meant for storage. It was flimsy but if she balanced her weight just right it would hold her. From her hiding spot she heard the noise again, a repetitive banging followed closely by the kicking in of her front door.

The voices of strange men filled her house, "Tear this place apart, every inch. I know they have our money. Take anything we can sell, smash anything that isn't worth it." And they did just that for more than an hour, often coming dangerously close to discovering Piper in her hiding spot. The mayhem had ended and the men had left, yet Piper remained crouched on the top shelf of her closet for the entire night, sobbing and shaking.

The next morning, with her eyes burning from salty tears and lack of sleep, she slid herself down and landed heavily on the floor. The pins and needles in her legs took a full five minutes to taper off. She crept through her house, looking at everything that had been broken or overturned, seeing empty spaces where things had been stolen. When the front door swung open, she jumped with fear, assuming the men had returned for her. Instead she was met with the strung out red eyes of her parents dragging themselves in from their last drug binge.

"What the hell did you do?" her father shouted, running his hands across his hair and pulling at it in that manic way that punctuated his mental fragility. Piper couldn't right herself. She couldn't come to terms with her fear, her anger, and then her desire to hug her parents out of gratefulness that they had returned. At nine years old, she still needed people, unable to make it on her own. But her only people were these *people, and it was impossible to balance the myriad of different emotions.*

"These men came," she said, her voice shaking with the emotions she was drowning in.

"And you just let them do this?" her mother asked, pointing around the room at the damage. "Why didn't you stop them?" she yelled, picking up a work boot that had been pulled from the closet and left by the door. She cocked it back and launched it at Piper who crossed her arms and covered her face. Her forearms took the brunt of the blow as she tumbled backward. She heard the stomping feet of her father crossing the floor and she braced herself for more.

Instead of feeling the thumping of his fists against her body, Piper felt the wet nose of Bruno nudging her.

She woke, the sweat beading on her neck and back. These damn dreams were not just frightening things to relive, they were forcing her to come to terms with the contradictions of her life, the confusion. How could she lie there, being beaten for not protecting her house from grown men and, on some level, still be happy? She was so relieved not to be alone, not to have been abandoned, that the wrath unleashed on her was something she almost welcomed.

This had been the third nightmare she'd had since coming to the cabin, and each time Bruno had woken her just before the most traumatic parts of her memories could flood in. He was a rescue dog, apparently even in dreams.

As she continued to shake off the fog of her dream and the complex feelings that came with it, Bruno lifted his head and sniffed the air. It was normally the first indication that he sensed something coming. Then his ears perked up, and Piper sat motionless, allowing him to do his job. He dismounted the couch and began to bark loudly at the door. Then headlights cut through the darkness of the long driveway, and once again Piper put her hand over the alarm system's panic button. But it only took her a moment to recognize the rumble of Bobby's engine as the shiny red truck pulled in. Unlike Betty's visit, Piper did not instantly call off Bruno's alert. She allowed him to bark loudly and growl, looking up occasionally at her for direction. Not until Bobby had his hand hesitantly ready to knock did she give Bruno the command to relax. She pulled open the door and, just as she had when Betty visited, initially stayed silent.

"I have some news, and I wanted you to hear it from me," Bobby said, aching to hold her and hoping she was feeling the same thing. They could be mad at each other, he understood that, but it didn't erase what they shared.

"I'm getting most of my news from Maria Santos now. You don't really need to fill me in. I already heard they confirmed it was my father," Piper shot back, annoyed by how happy she was to see Bobby.

"Maria's an idiot. Whoever her sources are, they're wrong. I just heard from Agent Carlson. The medical examiner and the forensics team have ruled your father out of the two attacks on campus. The weapon, the victimology, the scene—none of it point to your father. It's not him, Piper." Bobby was still standing in the doorway, hoping she'd invite him in. And hoping that monstrous dog wouldn't try to eat him.

"Thanks for coming by to let me know. Tell Agent Carlson I'm sorry she came down here for nothing and that she'll have to excuse me for not saying goodbye."

"She's convinced you should still take the offer of witness protection. Even if the news comes out tonight and announces they have ruled him out, it will still get sensationalized. He'll know you're here."

"It's so strange, I feel like I've heard this somewhere before," Piper said with a look of feigned confusion. "Oh that's right, this is what I told you would happen," she concluded forcefully.

"Do you need to hear you were right? Is that what you're waiting for?" Bobby had told himself he wouldn't get argumentative, he'd keep his voice calm, but he was faltering.

"No, I guess I'm waiting for the marshals to come pick me up again so I can start a new life somewhere else. Please tell Betty, Jules, and Michael it was a blast, but I can't see them anymore. And tell them I'm keeping the damn dog." Piper stepped into the house and slammed the door hard enough to have Bobby stumbling backward.

No, he thought, not a chance, Piper. He pulled the door open and let himself in the house, praying the dog wouldn't go right for his throat. He shouted, "I had an obligation."

"Please stop. We are never going to agree on this. I love you, Bobby. I let myself love you, and you chose your badge over me, so now I'm the one who's going to suffer."

"Do you think I haven't been suffering? I love you, too." He slammed his fist down on the table next to the door and Piper jumped. She hated when people did that, it immediately reminded her of her father. Bruno didn't seem to care for it either. He went from sitting comfortably next to Piper's firmly planted feet, to standing at attention. Bobby took notice of both of their reactions and calmed himself. "We can make this work."

"How do you propose we do that? Should I just stay here and wait for my father to show up? Look over my shoulder every time I'm at the grocery store or the gas station? I don't see how I can stay here. I have to leave."

"I agree," Bobby said, resignedly. "But I can go with you. I know you think I chose my career over you, that I was trying to be a big shot or further myself. I wasn't, I was worried for the safety of the people I'm sworn to protect. Let me prove it to you. Let me leave all of it behind and come with you."

"Sure, Bobby, let's get a package deal and take Betty, Jules, and Michael, too. They can't talk to their family or friends anymore because they have to start new lives. I'm sure they'd be real open to it. And don't think you just get to move to Idaho and you're a cop there too. It doesn't work like that. This isn't a vacation, you become whoever they tell you to be."

"Why are you fighting me so hard on this? Help me find a way to make this work." Bobby knew he didn't have the perfect solution but he wanted to find one together.

"You're thinking about the logistics of how to make this work. Don't you see there's a much bigger obstacle here than where we live, or what our names are? We are fundamentally different. We can't build a life if we can't even see eye to eye on the basic principles of right and wrong. There is nothing you can tell me that would convince me you did the right thing here, and there was nothing I could have said that would have stopped you. That's a recipe for disaster, and I've had enough disaster in my life. We can't make this work. I need you to give me my space. I need you to let me go. Just go."

Bobby's phone rang, and he ignored it, his eyes locked on Piper's. He half hoped they'd be filled with tears but her chin was high and her shoulders back. She meant what she was saying. As he started to speak Piper's phone rang, and she also ignored it. Then his rang again, and their locked eyes changed from annoyance to worry.

"Did Michael just call you?" Bobby asked, now looking down at his phone. Piper grabbed hers and nodded her head in confirmation. "He's calling me again," Bobby said, putting the phone to his ear.

"What's up, Michael?" Bobby asked, still trying to read Piper's face for any sign that she may come over to his side. He stood silently, listening for several moments with furrowed brows as he attempted to understand what Michael was saying. "Slow down, how long has she been gone?" He paused again, and Piper could feel her heart thudding in her chest. This was bad news, she knew this was bad news. "That's just how she is, Michael, trust me. I know her like the back of my hand. She runs off whenever things don't go her way. I haven't had a chance to fill you in yet, but the FBI says the attacks on campus aren't linked to the Railway Killer, so that should ease your mind a bit. I don't think we have any imminent danger. I'm sure she'll be back soon." Bobby was now rolling his eyes at Piper as though he couldn't believe how much Michael was blowing things out of proportion.

"No," interrupted Piper shaking her head. "You don't know Jules like the back of your hand. You think she's this emotional train wreck, but she's trying really hard to be better. I don't think she would have just run off tonight. How long has it been since he's heard from her?"

"About six hours. She isn't answering her cell phone and he's already checked with Betty," Bobby mouthed to Piper, his phone still at his ear as Michael continued to insist something was wrong. Piper looked sternly at Bobby, not satisfied with his opinion. Feeling outnumbered once again, Bobby relented with a sigh and responded to Michael. "Okay, I'll call into the station and put an alert out for her. I'll drive around a couple of her favorite haunts to see if she's pouting anywhere. You stay at your place, and let me know when she comes back, because trust me, she's coming back."

Bobby hung up his phone and tucked it back in his pocket, cursing Jules for the distraction. He couldn't remember now where the conversation with Piper was heading, or how he was going to convince her that they'd weather any storm as long as they were together. Now he had to go do what he had done for the last ten years—take care of Jules.

"Come with me," Bobby pleaded. "We aren't finished talking. I'm not ready for this to be over."

She wasn't sure if he meant their relationship or the conversation, but really she didn't care. They were both over for her. She had spent days convincing herself of that and preparing an effort to minimize the sting that would come from inevitably having to say goodbye to all of them. When Piper didn't agree, he took another angle. "If Jules really is upset, it's you she'll want to talk to. I'll just screw it up."

"Well the odds are in your favor for that." Piper looked down at Bruno as if to ask his opinion. Clearly he was indifferent. "Fine," she said reluctantly, "but only because I'm worried about Jules. The dog is coming with us." She reached down and rubbed the spot behind Bruno's ear that always made him happily lean into her.

Bruno became a physical barrier between Bobby and Piper in the front seat of his truck. His big, furry body perched between them to the point where they could barely see each other, and that was fine by Piper. She was adding this to the list of things Bruno did that made her like him. He was lessening the sting from the conflict she felt being back in Bobby's truck. This had always been a safe place where she could let her mind relax, knowing Bobby was in control. But now the truck made her feel trapped.

Piper stared out the window, letting silence settle between them as they drove the streets of downtown Edenville. It was a thick silence, like a bubble slowly filling the truck and pushing them further apart.

It had been nice to be away from all the hypocrisy in downtown Edenville for the last few days. The cabin was depressingly quiet at times, but at least there were no fake smiling faces. She had no problem leaving a place with picturesque façades hiding such dark secrets. At least back home in Brooklyn you knew what you were getting. Staring up at the broken windows of the cement high-rise projects she grew up in left little room for imagination. You didn't sit out front and wonder if the next Pulitzer Prize winner was penning a novel in there. That place didn't try to fool anyone. It wasn't trying to be something it wasn't. It looked as depressing as it was.

But as they drove past the diner and Town Hall she felt her heart tug a little. Every place had its black spots, but at least this place held some happy memories, too.

"So I checked in at the diner, and Town Hall is all locked up. We've been driving for two hours. I'm sure she doesn't want to be found at this point." Bobby wasn't annoyed that he'd run his gas tank nearly empty or that his back was starting to ache. He was aggravated that in the last two hours Piper hadn't cracked. She was holding tight to her all-business expression and limiting the conversation to Jules. The heat of Bruno's breath on his neck was the only sign of life in the truck at times. If two hours of driving around in his truck together, something she used to love to do, hadn't softened her, then two more hours certainly wasn't going to do it. And if he was being honest there was a small pinch of worry that kept creeping in. Maybe Agent Carlson had ruled out the Railway Killer, but there could still be a copycat out there. He did his best to keep dismissing the fear. Jules was just being Jules.

"Let's keep looking," she whispered, staring out into the night. Maybe it was just her drive to find Jules, or maybe, Bobby hoped, she wasn't quite ready to leave him yet.

Chapter Ten

JULES WOKE SLOWLY. She felt hung over but couldn't recall a fun night of drinking to explain the feeling. Without opening her eyes, she fought through the fuzziness clouding her brain. Something was very wrong. She could feel she was lying on hard ground and something prickly was poking her in the back. She tried to reach behind her to see what it was but quickly realized she couldn't move her right arm more than a couple inches. Why was her arm stuck?

She dared to open her eyes and lift her aching head. The sudden throbbing in her leg made her forget about her restrained arm. As her eyes struggled to focus in the dim moonlight, she saw that her jeans were sliced open horizontally and blood had begun to dry and harden tightly on her skin. She swallowed hard, pushing back the terrified lump in her throat. Still unable to move her right arm, she used the sleeve of her left arm to wipe gingerly at the wound. She sucked in a rattling breath as she saw that the source of her pain was a neatly carved number twenty-five in her thigh. In an instant, like the walls were falling in on her, she understood what this meant.

She beat back the urge to scream and called upon every bit of strength she could muster. She was becoming a new Jules for a reason. She was giving up the impulsive, emotionally driven reactions of her youth. Piper was inspiring her through her troubled past to find courage and gratitude for everything she had. She must stay calm; in moments like this, remaining in control of her emotions would be crucial. She closed her eyes again and thought back to her father's many lessons on protecting herself. As the daughter of a police officer, Jules's lessons in safety went far beyond the typical "look both ways before crossing the street" and "don't ever get into a car with a stranger" talks most parents gave their children. Although she had often scoffed at what had seemed to be her father's overly precautious lectures, she was suddenly very grateful that he had told her what to do if she were ever kidnaped or held hostage.

She assessed the situation and her surroundings. Her left arm was free but her right was handcuffed to a wood beam. The cold air was making her cheeks tingle. It was dark, but a rusted lantern hung from another beam about ten yards from her, its yellow light casting eerie shadows. Jules could tell she was in an old barn that, judging by its state of disrepair, hadn't been used in years. She shifted her body and realized it was straw that was poking her in the back. She could smell rich earth, not manure, just healthy cultivated land. She was on some kind of farm, likely abandoned. She closed her eyes and listened for any noises. There were crickets chirping loudly just outside the barn. Off in the distance she heard the rumbling of engines, eighteen-wheelers. She must be close to the highway. Judging by how frequently she heard the roaring of the Jake brakes there must be a good-size hill forcing the trucks to slow down with their heavy loads. She was frantically searching for other clues, not sure when she would use them or how she could benefit from them, but at least it was keeping her mind from spiraling to the terror attempting to overcome her.

She tugged at her chained arm. The beam was solid, the cuff was tight, and there was nothing within reach that could help her escape it. Her phone was no longer in her pocket. What were her options here? She whispered to herself, "What am I going to do? Think, think."

She felt the breath in her lungs turn to stone and the hair on her neck rise as a man stepped into view. He stood with the light of the lantern glowing behind him, a daunting silhouette standing ominously just feet from her.

"What a stupid question. You don't get to do anything, that's the point." The man's voice was gravelly and low. Exactly how you'd imagine a serial killer would talk. He took two enormous steps toward Jules who was frozen with fear, her eyes wide and locked on him. "Do you know how badly I want to kill you?" he roared, as he paced back and forth in front of Jules. In his hand he juggled a rusty but sharp spike. His movements were like sparks, nervous, sputtering, and twitching.

Jules thought quickly back to all of her father's advice. Be human, connect with the person. Let the captor know you are someone's daughter, someone's friend. She licked at her dry lips and mustered every ounce of courage to speak. "I'm sorry you're so upset," she said just above a whisper. "There are people who can help you feel better."

He lunged forward and crouched down in front of her. He growled into her face. "I already know what makes me feel better. It's watching some bitch gasp for her last breath."

Unable to hide her fear, Jules shakily tried another approach. "They are going to catch you," she said as defiantly as she could through her tears.

He cackled a terrifying laugh into her face, and she felt the heat of his breath on her cheeks. "She doesn't want to catch me. She brought me here. She wants me to kill my daughter so I can start all over again. You think she's one of the good guys, but she can't live if she isn't chasing me."

"Who?" Jules asked, trying to make sense of the ranting.

"Oh, you're so stupid," he barked, running the tip of the spike over her cheek. "Why would she send me those messages, attack those girls right here in the town where I can find my daughter? She knows I can't kill anyone else until Isabella is dead, so she led me right to her. She knows why I do this, she wants me to kill."

"Why do you do this?" Jules wasn't sure what approach would work for this man. Likely there wouldn't be one. He was a deranged madman with nothing to connect to, but if she was asking questions, at least she was still alive.

"Every single woman I have ever killed has deserved it. They've laughed at me, walked away from me. They think they are better than me. They think they can just ignore me. Well they have plenty to say, plenty to beg for, when I'm standing over them while they bleed. My bitch of a wife and ungrateful daughter thought they could do the same thing. They thought they could leave me. They made a mistake, and now I need to finish what I started. She can't be walking around, she can't." He stood abruptly, clearly enraged at the mere thought of his daughter being alive. "And when I do drain the blood from her body, when I do finally kill her, you'll know you're next. I'll hunt you." He planted his booted foot down onto her thigh next to the carved number twenty-five, and she cried out in pain.

"Why not just kill me now?" Jules asked, pursing her lips together and glaring at the man. "If you're such a monster, such a powerful man, then why don't you just kill me right now? Or are you really that weak that you can't even control your own mind?" Jules watched in awe as the man wrestled with himself, quickly standing upright and slapping the spike to his forehead. He spoke frantically in a low voice as he paced in erratic circles.

"Shut up!" he finally shouted, talking more to the voices in his head than to Jules, though she jumped, tugging again at the chain on her arm. He pulled her pink phone from his pocket and tossed it down to her. She scrambled for it, looking confused, but dialing anyway.

"I can't deliver a message if no one comes to pick up the package," he mused, his tone now calm as though he had righted himself back to the course he had originally planned. "You're her friend, she'll know what this means. She'll know her time is running out. And more than that, she'll know I'm going to kill you next." His voice had turned to the hiss of a snake, a victorious chant.

Jules put the phone to her ear, keeping her eyes on her captor in distrust. She couldn't believe he was letting her call for help. Hearing the familiar nasal voice of Melisa the dispatcher, Jules burst into tears. "911, what is your emergency?" Melisa asked. Jules watched as the man pulled a bag over his shoulder and disappeared out the door of the barn.

"Melisa, it's Jules. I've been kidnapped." Whatever

composure she had pulled together to face this monster was now gone. Her adrenaline was the only thing keeping her from completely succumbing to terror. "I need every officer you have and an ambulance out here." She fumbled over her words, her voice quaking.

"Jules, okay I hear you, can you tell me where you are?"

"I think I'm off highway forty-one. I'm in an abandoned barn about a hundred yards from the road. I think it must be one of the farms that shut down after the highway came through. I can hear trucks hitting their brakes, so there must be a big hill. There aren't too many of them on that stretch of highway. I'm not positive, I'm just guessing. Can you trace my phone?"

"I'm doing it now," Melisa said calmly. "It should give us your location within a half mile. Between that and the information you just gave us we'll find you. Are you in any immediate danger?"

"He left, he's gone I think, but I don't know if he's coming back. Please just hurry." The tears were coming fast now, her cheeks soaked. Melisa muted the line for a moment and leaned over to her partner. "Gabby, you better get Bobby on the phone. I've got Jules on the line here and she's in some kind of trouble." Switching back over to Jules she regained her calm demeanor. "Jules I have your closest cell tower now, and I have officers en route. They'll be there soon, sweetie, just hold tight."

Chapter Eleven

BOBBY USED HIS shoulder to hold his cell phone to his ear as he made a quick and illegal U-turn. The six hours Jules had been missing had turned into eight and then finally an urgent call from dispatch had deflated Bobby's blustery arrogance. He had been wrong. This wasn't a Jules temper-tantrum. This was serious. "What hospital are they taking her to?" Bobby's voice was layered with panic, something he rarely showed. Piper reached her arm across the seat in front of Bruno and put her hand on his leg, trying to steady him emotionally and brace herself as well. "I'll have Michael pick up Betty and we'll meet there."

"What is it?" Piper asked, her eyes wide with fear.

"I couldn't get all the details. I just know from guys on the scene that she was alert and talking. She told them it was your—the Railway Killer that took her." He couldn't bring himself to say, *your father,* to Piper. "She said she's positive it was him. It doesn't make any sense. The FBI ruled him out. She's at St. Catherine's Hospital. I'm sure she's okay now, she has to be." Bobby reached down for Piper's hand that was still resting on his leg, and he laced his fingers with hers.

"She's okay, Bobby," Piper said reassuringly. "She's going to be fine." That seemed like the right thing to say in that moment, but really Piper wasn't sure. She knew what her father was capable of and she knew how hard it was to recover, physically and mentally, from his torment.

Bobby pulled his truck to the front of the hospital and they leapt out, ignoring the no parking sign. Bruno followed obediently. With any luck a tow truck would recognize the pickup as Bobby's and cut him a break. If not, he didn't care.

He needed to get to Jules.

Michael and Betty were racing into the hospital right behind Piper, Bobby, and Bruno. They were both ghost white and their eyes darted frantically as they all reached the front desk. Recognizing the nurse on duty as a regular customer of hers at the diner, Betty wasted no time.

"Where is she, Meryl? Where is my baby?" Betty cried.

"The FBI is in with her right now. They requested we don't let anyone in until they're finished. And you can't have a dog in here." The voluptuous nurse had her hands on her hips, staring down at Bruno, letting Betty know she meant business.

"I don't care if Jesus Christ himself is in there, no one is keeping me from my child. Tell me what room she is in."

"I'm sorry, Betty, if I could, I would, you know that." Meryl tried to soften her face, hoping to let Betty know she felt bad but she had a job to do. She knew Betty to be a formidable woman rarely taking no for an answer, but the FBI had been very clear.

"You tell me where my daughter is or I will tell everyone in this town what you did with you know who."

"You wouldn't!" Meryl said, covering her heart with her hands. Betty raised a goading eyebrow, challenging Meryl to call her bluff.

"Fine, she's in room 221, but you best not tell them I told you." Meryl crossed her arms over her chest like a pouting child who'd just been sent off to bed without dessert.

"I wouldn't dream of it, Meryl, you know I can keep a secret." Betty returned to her charming smile, and Meryl huffed at the irony the statement. "And the dog can't go in there!" she called as the group hustled down the hall. She cursed under her breath as they ignored her and disappeared around a corner.

They made their way to the room Jules was in and burst through the door, all four of them looking haggard and worried but relieved to see Jules sitting up with just a large bandage on her thigh.

"Oh, my baby," Betty howled, running to her side and wrapping her arms tightly around her daughter.

"Excuse me, Mrs. Grafton, my name is Agent Lydia Carlson, and I'm sorry to interrupt, but you can't be in here right now. We need to get your daughter's statement." Carlson looked at each person who had just barged in and gave an odd look at the dog trailing in behind. "Frankly, considering the circumstances, she's lucky to be alive." Agent Carlson turned toward Piper and spoke calculatedly in her direction. "I'm not sure how many more warnings I can give about the seriousness of this. I don't know how much more blood you intend to get on those hands of yours."

Bruno, who was now standing by Piper's feet, let out a low growl. No teeth showing, no aggressive stance, just a quiet warning. Agent Carlson looked down at the dog again and then back up at Piper who whispered, "He's a great judge of character."

Betty stepped back from her daughter and spun on Agent Carlson until they were nose to nose. She'd heard enough about this bully. Each encounter and every phone call she'd overheard that involved this woman was toxic. It was time to nip it in the bud with a good ole fashioned tongue-lashing.

"Lydia," she said firmly, surprising everyone in the room. Betty was probably the only person who could get away with calling a federal agent by her first name and manage to sound full of authority as she did it. "Don't you think for a second I don't know what makes a woman like you tick, because I do." Betty's finger was pointed now like a dagger nearly poking Carlson in the eye. "You've given your whole life to that badge, and we're all grateful for your service. But now you're getting on in years and there ain't nobody calling you mama, nobody holding the other half of your heart. That makes a hole in a person that can't be filled by nothing but other people's pain. You want to go around out there," Betty said pointing at the door, "trying to tear people down, you go right ahead. But these people, here in this room, these are my people, and you won't speak to them like that again." Carlson wrinkled her brows in disbelief and opened her mouth to speak, but Betty cut her off.

"And don't be looking at me like I'm breaking the law and threatening you here. I ain't talking about taking you into the parking lot and whooping you like your mama should have. I'm too old for that. You see, here in the South, we'll just find what you love, whatever thing that keeps that sad, broken heart of yours ticking every day, and we'll snatch it from you before you even see us coming. That's how we take care of things. Are we clear?"

"Crystal." Agent Carlson's eyes were as wide as saucers as she responded. It was all she could manage to say, too stunned to engage Betty any further. Her hand shook slightly and she stuffed it into her pocket, hoping the tremor had gone unnoticed. She hadn't been talked to like that since... well... ever.

"Now, baby," Betty said, turning back toward Jules as though nothing had happened, "can I get you something?"

"I'm real thirsty, Ma, could you get me some water?" Jules asked, fighting a smile. She was brimming over with pride for her mother's strength. She'd seen her mother fight countless battles like this before and win effortlessly. She certainly had a way with words.

"Lydia," Betty said, smiling with her Southern charm. "I'm guessing you won't be here when I get back, so you take care now."

Agent Carlson nodded and half smiled back at Betty, feeling sheepishly small in this room of people who were probably all laughing inside at her expense. "Jules," she said, regaining her ability to speak, "so you are, without any doubt, able to identify the man who took you as Roberto Lee Lawson, the Railway Killer. However you're telling me he didn't say anything to you?"

"Not a word," Jules confirmed. "I'm really very tired, Agent Carlson," she continued with true weariness in her voice. "I'd like some time with my friends and a chance to rest. If I think of anything else, I'll let you know."

Again at a loss for words, Agent Carlson nodded her head, put her pen back in her breast pocket, and quietly exited the room. The group remaining all looked at each other silently in disbelief over the uncharacteristically quiet Carlson. Then they quickly turned their attention to Jules.

"I'm so sorry," Michael said, pulling the chair next to her bed and holding her hand. "I shouldn't have let you go off like that."

"It's not your fault, Michael. We can talk about it after. Right now I have to tell you guys what Piper's father said to me." Everyone in the room was stunned. They had just heard Jules tell Carlson that no words had passed between her and the killer.

"Jules," Bobby snapped, "you have to tell Carlson everything you know. She is in charge of the investigation, and she needs all the information possible to try to catch him. I know we don't like her, but that's not enough reason to obstruct the case."

"Can you please get over yourself, Bobby?" It wasn't a question, but a demand. Jules was completely exasperated by his high and mighty tone. "We get it, you're a cop. Put the damn rule book away for five minutes and give me the benefit of the doubt here." Part of Bobby was growing tired of hearing this, but the other part was wondering if maybe they were right about him. He sank his shoulders down and closed his mouth.

Piper, the only person in the room yet to talk, finally found her voice. "What did he say? How did he sound?"

"He sounded like a lunatic," Jules admitted. "I'm sorry if that's hard to hear, I just mean he sounded really manic. Like he's about to go over the edge. He was upset that he couldn't kill me. Their theory is right, he is here for you. He can't deviate from whatever makes him kill, and he needs you dead to be able to kill again."

"That cut on your leg, is it what I think it is?" Piper asked, unable to look away from the bandage.

"It's the number twenty-five," Jules said, trying unsuccessfully to keep all emotion out of her voice. She had held herself together the best she could in order to convey the horrific night's events, but now that she was surrounded by those who loved her most, she was dangerously close to breaking down. "He was sending you a message. Once he kills you, he plans to hunt me down and... kill me," she finished in a near whisper.

"He isn't going to kill either of you," Michael interjected firmly, protectively responding to the fear in both Jules's voice and Piper's eyes.

"Listen, none of that matters right now," Jules continued, gathering her strength and resolve once again. "He went off on this rant about how *she* doesn't want to catch him. That *she* is the one who brought him here. Those attacks on campus weren't his doing. They were meant to be a road map here. I think Agent Carlson wanted him to find Piper, I think she wanted him to turn up in Edenville."

Bobby shook his head, annoyed by the theory. "Agent Carlson has been with the FBI for years. There is no way she wants to see Piper killed or wants a serial killer to take out the one person stopping him from killing more people."

"No," Michael said, as the pieces began to fall into place in his head, "but she does want him caught. He's been dormant for two years. Everyone knows the best way to catch a killer is to find evidence at crime scenes. That's where they make their mistakes, where the break in the case normally comes from. When there are no crime scenes, the trail goes cold. I'm sure Carlson doesn't want Piper killed, but I would believe that she'd use her for bait. She was pretty passive in her push for witness protection. If she'd really wanted to, she could have had Piper placed back into witness protection just from the original agreement they signed. She'd be legally justified in doing so. Perhaps she got tired of a cold trail and—"

"And what?" Bobby interjected, still skeptical that someone with that type of job could stoop so low. "Do you think she attacked two defenseless girls on campus just to draw him here? Do you think she leaked to the press that the surviving victim was here in Edenville? Are we really considering accusing her of that?"

"I'm not considering accusing her of anything," Michael said defensively. "I'm suggesting that we work under the assumption that she did those things, and therefore we don't trust her. Piper, if you were considering going back into witness protection, I don't think you should. If Carlson is involved in any way it won't matter where you go. If she knows where you are, you won't be safe."

Jules nodded her head in agreement and looked over at Bobby for some kind of read on his opinion as Michael continued to speak. "Bobby, I know you want to believe that it's not possible for someone with a badge to have a hidden agenda, but look at what we went through with Rylie and the judge. These people are out there. They exist. We need to go off the grid for a little while, somewhere Carlson can't track us and we can all take a few deep breaths and regroup. Do you have any idea where we could go?"

Bobby looked around the room at these people. They were constantly testing him and challenging his efforts to keep his past at bay, to right his own wrongs. He wanted to tell them all to butt out and let him do his job the way he was trained to do it. But he couldn't deny agreeing that they needed to regroup, and he did know one place they could go and all be safe. He had a favor he could call in. And the one redeeming thought of leaving for a while was at least he'd be with Piper. She'd be forced to talk to him at some point. If they were ever going to make amends, the close quarters might help.

"I've got a place we can go. It'll have plenty of security, and no one will be able to track us. I need to make a phone call. I'm sure you'll be here at least overnight, Jules. We should plan on leaving sometime after dark tomorrow." He paused and saw Michael squeezing Jules's hand.

"Michael, I know you have work. We'll be safe where we're going. You're off the hook if you need to hang back."

"I'm coming." He pulled Jules's hand up to his lips and kissed it. Without taking his eyes off her he told Bobby, "Just make your phone call and let's get out of here."

Chapter Twelve

IT HAD TAKEN a little tactful strong arming, Betty's specialty, to get Jules released from the hospital the next evening. They had quickly packed bags and loaded Michael's car under the dark of night. They hadn't had much time to sleep. They had taken turns, someone staying with Jules while the others went and prepared for the trip. Michael, much to Piper's disappointment, had returned Bruno to his trainer. There was just no room for him on a road trip. Piper had grown surprisingly attached to the dog, and saying goodbye wasn't easy. Bruno made her feel safe, and his ability to wake her from her vivid nightmares had become something she depended on.

Bobby had tended to everything at Betty's house and his own. He and Piper still hadn't said much to each other. The fear of losing Jules had made their argument feel trivial at times, but then something would happen, someone would say something that would remind them they stood on opposite sides. Betty asked if Bobby had talked to Agent Carlson again, and Piper made a snarky remark about her being on his speed-dial. The tension fell and rose like the tide, and neither knew when it would settle or flare. It was like a wound, and every time it started to heal over, something would tear it open again.

Bobby and Michael decided they would drive through the night in shifts, leaving the rest of the group to drift in and out of uncomfortable sleep.

"So wait a minute, who is this guy we're going to stay with?" Jules asked, trying to adjust her leg comfortably in the front seat of Michael's car. She wasn't excited about having an injury to her leg, but on a thirteen-hour road trip it did ensure her the front seat, and that was a plus.

Michael, who had volunteered for the first driving shift, looked in his rearview mirror at Bobby, suggesting he answer the complex question.

He opted for answering Jules's question with a matter-of-fact approach. There wasn't really a way to sugarcoat it, so he dove right in. "We're going to stay with Christian Donovan."

"Seriously? Isn't he like a major criminal?" Jules asked, hoping this was some kind of a joke. Were they really running away from one crime-ridden family straight to another? Piper was less surprised by Bobby's answer. She knew Bobby didn't have a long list of people to ask for a favor like this and she'd figured there was a chance Christian was the person he'd be calling.

"He was a criminal. But remember we told you he had decided to turn over all the evidence he had in exchange for witness protection? Well, he was relocated to Illinois. We're heading to the Midwest." Bobby said this last sentence with forced enthusiasm as if he'd said, "We're going to Disney World!" the way a quarterback might in post Super Bowl tradition. Seeing that his optimism was clearly wasted on these people, he returned to his normal voice. "He's a complicated guy, but the information and evidence he provided helped tremendously. I think we can trust him."

"So he's a rat?" Jules asked, frowning at the vision in her head of a gold-chained bald informant like one might see in a movie.

"I highly recommend you don't say that when we get there," Michael interjected. Bobby agreed, "Yeah, I'm pretty sure that wouldn't sit well with him. Like I said, he's complicated. He has an eight-year-old son. He wanted a better life for him than the one he had growing up. Christian didn't exactly choose his lifestyle—it was kind of a self-fulfilling prophecy. He was looking for an opportunity to get out, and we presented him with one. Because of that, he feels like he owes us his life. This is his way of paying off his debt."

Jules still looked unconvinced, and turned to Michael, raising her eyebrows. "You really think we can trust him? You talk about him like you know him." Michael couldn't help but look sheepish. The truth was, he had been in contact with Christian since his relocation, and he did feel he'd gotten to know him reasonably well. At first, Christian had contacted Michael, hoping to stay abreast of how things were unfolding in Edenville following the takedown of Judge Lions. Michael knew maintaining communications with Christian was wrong, and, more than that, he knew Bobby wouldn't approve, but he just couldn't say no. He heard the desperation in Christian's voice, the battle he was having with himself. Christian had done something some would see as heroic, others as betrayal, and it was clear his own mind danced between those two ideas. Keeping him informed of the prosecutions and retrials was the least Michael could do. When Bobby revealed the plan to drive to Illinois to stay with Christian, Michael had admitted to keeping in touch with the ex-criminal. As expected, his confession was met with Bobby's wary, disappointed grimace, but the urgency of the situation at hand had trumped his frustration and saved Michael from a lecture.

In an attempt to avoid explaining all of this to the rest of the group, Michael asked a question he'd been putting off until they were on the road. This way whatever the answer was, Piper couldn't back out. "And what about baby brother Sean, we're not going to have to deal with him, are we?"

"He's currently being treated in a rehab and counseling facility, just like Christian promised. He's trying to get him some help," Bobby said, almost apologetically to Piper. They had both tried to minimize the danger Piper had been in that night that Christian's brother, Sean, had slipped a Rohypnol into her drink. She had been playing detective that night, but Sean had other plans in mind. If not for Michael, who knows what would have happened? It was a good thing Sean wouldn't be around, because it would be nearly impossible for him not to have his ass kicked by any one of them.

"That's quite the family," Betty chimed in. "I knew their

grandmother. When I was in my twenties I used to fill in at my aunt's bridge club occasionally, and Mrs. Donavan frequently hosted. She used to tell stories about how her son was hell on wheels from the time he was ten years old. I'm amazed he was even able to raise those boys into adulthood at all. I'm not surprised they ended up on the wrong side of the law. I hope they do better in this new life. I recall there were a lot of unanswered questions around their parents' death—the tragedy of them dying together like that, husband and wife murdered. I guess that's what happens when you get mixed up in that world."

"Boy, this should be fun," Jules said, rolling her eyes at Michael. "So we're going to be house guests of some felon."

"It's our best option right now, Jules. No one knows where he is, no one knows we have any ties to him, and he won't be counting on witness protection to keep him safe. He'll have his own security. Oh, that reminds me, his new name is Chris King. His son goes by little Chris."

"They didn't make them change their first names?" Piper asked, remembering how much she had initially despised her new name and how firm they had been that she had no choice in the matter.

"I asked him that, and he said they did give him a different name, Herman, I think. He said there was no way he was walking around the rest of his life with that name. So he went out and got fake IDs made with the name he wanted. He said he was trying to minimize the impact on his son. I'm sure they really love him over in witness protection."

The drive to Joliet, Illinois from Edenville was a long one, made longer by frequent stops. Bobby and Michael both found themselves annoyed by the lack of coordination of the bladders in the car. They were sounding like overbearing parents, insisting the girls remaining in the car at least go *try* to use the bathroom, because they didn't intend to stop again for another three hours.

For Piper, riding in Michael's car meant she'd need to fight sleep, afraid of what might be waiting for her there. But inevitably she gave in to her need for rest, and just as she had feared, her memories were lurking there.

It was a visit. A knock on the door making waves in already turbulent water. One afternoon the proverbial stars aligned creating the absolute worst-case scenario. Some brave souls, Catholic priests, decided they'd bring their gospel to the projects. It was well-intentioned, but ultimately a misguided endeavor. The rap on the door was uncharacteristically upbeat for anything you'd hear in their world. In the projects you don't tap, you bang on a door.

Her mother was out, working some minimum wage job that she'd inevitably get fired from. So the role of opening the door would fall on her. At the sight of the two young men with their crisp black shirts and white collars she froze. It was like watching oblivious animals marched to slaughter. Their wide smiles and meek demeanors were not comforting to Piper, but terrifying. She was afraid for them, not of them. Men like this, men of God as she had heard them called, didn't belong in a place with so much hate.

She didn't greet them, she just let her surprised eyes ask the questions. Luckily this wasn't the first apartment they'd been to in her building, so they were prepared for the shock. "Hello sweetheart," one of the men started, handing her a pamphlet, which she reluctantly took. His Irish accent was as thick as honey. She'd never heard a real person speak like this before. He sounded like the leprechaun on that cereal commercial always looking for his lucky charms. It almost made the corner of her mouth curl into a smile, but she quickly reconsidered. "We're here today to speak to you about Jesus Christ. Do you know who that is?"

She did. She'd heard of him. She knew a little bit about religion from what her father had occasionally rambled on about in drug-induced moments he considered "clarity." He called it a sermon and it would either be about religion, politics, or a conspiracy theory he'd dreamt up. It was his version of a life lesson for her; the only problem was, none of it ever made sense.

As the two men at her door made no move to leave, she looked over her shoulder, toward where she had left her father asleep on the couch. He was gone now. He appeared quickly from the bedroom where he went to retrieve his pants. That was a positive she guessed, at least he'd have his pants on when he kicked these people out. But that wasn't at all what happened. Her father was high, but not his normal high or drunk demeanor. He and her mother had come into a little money, though Piper didn't have the details of how they acquired it. This didn't mean more food, or clothes, or any other basic necessities. No, this meant special-occasion drugs. They had their basic addictions, which they scrapped money together to support. However, when they had a windfall of any kind it meant they'd splurge.

This time it was a sheet of acid. She'd seen her father tear off a square and put it in his mouth about a half hour before the knock on the door. If history was any indication, this meant the effects should be taking hold of him now. The crushing panic started to overtake her. She wanted to shout for the men at her door to go away and slam it tightly, not wanting them to see the mortifying results of her father tripping. Would he lick the walls this time, claiming they were chocolate? Would he strip down naked again and attempt to scale the building, not making it more than a foot off the ground?

"Who do we have here?" her father asked, approaching the door. The men were unaware of what synthetic factors were making him sound so welcoming.

"Hello sir," they said in unison, offering her father a pamphlet, which he happily took from them. The taller man with the Irish accent had the wildest mop of curly red hair she'd ever seen. He was no more than twenty-five years old and likely considered this trip to the projects a religious mission. No different than spending time in South America or Africa. "We're here today to talk to you about our Lord and Savior. Do you

have time for us to share the good news with you?"

"Please come in," her father sang. Piper's jaw dropped as her father made a welcoming hand motion and pulled her back from the door to allow them room to enter. The men politely perched on the dirty couch with its missing springs and lumpy cushions. Her father sat across from them on a fluffy floral print chair that they had pulled from the dumpster behind their apartment. He gestured for Piper to sit by him on the arm of it. These men didn't seem to mind the condition of the apartment. They weren't judging. They were just so happy to have been given the opportunity to preach something they believed in.

The conversation went on for ten minutes, all fairly normal, much to Piper's surprise. Then she recognized the switch in her father, flipping like it had so many times before. His mind wasn't his own now, reality had split away.

"So," he asked, shaking his legs anxiously, "do you think anything is forgivable? Does God really just give you a pass if you ask for one?"

The men seemed to light up at this question. It was the cornerstone of what they believed in. Redemption was their selling point. "We do believe that," the shorter of the two men said, smiling.

"Even something really awful? Like what if you bought a tiger and you starved it, then turned it loose in a school? What if you sprinkled cocaine in random people's mashed potatoes and then called the police and ruined their lives? Could God forgive you if you locked all the doors and burned your building down?"

The men sat silent as they watched her father twitch, his body seeming to convert to something other than human. They searched his face trying to decide if he was attempting to make fools of them or if he was, perhaps, mentally unstable. The red-haired man stood, the other taking his lead and attempting to do the same, but her father lunged forward, and with a hand on his shoulder, forced him to stay seated and encouraged the other man to sit back down. He reluctantly obliged, clearly not *comfortable with where this was heading.*

For two hours and ten minutes her father, passively, kept the men hostage. He was asking ridiculous philosophical questions and forcing them to answer, even when the answer made no sense. She watched her father break down in tears, acting as though he'd been saved then flash with rage when he'd forget exactly what they had been speaking about or why they were there.

Piper watched the men oscillate between fear and sadness as they occasionally looked over at her. She had her hands folded in her lap, her shoulders drawn and drooping. They seemed to realize this was her life, her real life. For them it was just a story they would tell about the crazy man they'd tried to preach to that day. But this was how she lived every day, and probably would for a long time. Her father seemed to grow tired for a moment so she took her chance and attempted to intervene.

"Dad," she whispered, cutting into his frantic words. "I think they have to go to the next apartment now." He turned his head so quickly toward her that she thought it might snap right off his shoulders. She knew interrupting him would not be well-received, but she thought it was time to take a shot at it. She was wrong. His hand came up and she felt a sharp slap hit her face, knocking her off the arm of the chair and onto the floor. She heard the audible disgust from the men sitting across from her. If only they knew it actually hadn't hurt, she'd been much more accustomed to a closed-fist punch. The slap was not as bad as she had expected when she saw his arm rise.

"Sir!" the young Irish priest shouted. He moved across the small room and lifted Piper back to her feet. He stood in front of her like a shield. He smelled of incense, and his clothes were so crisply pressed they stayed pristinely neat even as he moved. There was something about this man that, for an instant, made her feel safe, an emotion so foreign to her that it felt like lightning bolts running through her. "Do you really think that was necessary?"

Her father stood as well, towering over the man. Piper

thought a brawl might ensue and these men were at a clear disadvantage. But much to her surprise, her father smiled. "Spare the rod, spoil the child." The moment of silence that hung in the room was excruciating. She watched as the young priest's face turned the same color as his hair. He clearly wanted to do something, say something, but nothing came to him.

"Thank you for coming by," Piper said quietly, smiling as her pink cheek stung. That was their opportunity to leave. There was hesitation as the two men looked back and forth between her and each other. Her father had flopped back down on the couch and was lacing his boots, and then quickly pulling the laces back out.

He was chanting words that sounded like a song she used to know, but nothing she could make sense of. She walked with the men to the door, ushering them away. "I don't want to leave ya here. Is there anyone we can call to help ya? Your ma, maybe?" Again his Irish singsong voice warmed her slightly even in the face of the trouble she had ahead of her.

"There's no one to help. Not when you live here. My mom will be home soon, but you wouldn't want to meet her either."

The man's eyes filled slightly with the shadow of tears. And even though it was she who would face much more pain in her life, Piper felt bad for the priest. He pulled a card from his pocket and placed it in her hand.

"If you ever need anything, please call me."

"Don't ever come back here," she said, the tears in her eyes now, too. "Please."

She made her way back from the door, trying to walk as quietly as possible. "That was crazy," her father said, running his hands through his wild hair. "Can you believe that? We can do whatever we want and God will forgive us. That is—that is just amazing." He was laughing now, cackling in a way Piper knew meant trouble. She thought maybe she could slip away to her room, shut the door, and wait for his high to subside, but luck was not on her side. She felt him grab a handful of her hair and tug her backward toward the couch. "I want to test this. We should test this." He lit a cigarette and pulled in a deep drag, letting the end burn bright orange.

"Come here, come over here." He patted the couch next to him. She reluctantly sat. He grabbed her thin wrist and yanked up her sleeve exposing the soft skin of her tiny arm. Her conscious mind was creeping in and she knew what came next. She still had the small raised round scar that came from that burn. Her father had wanted to do something wrong and then ask for God's forgiveness. That was his test.

"No, Dad, it burns! Please stop!" she shouted, flailing her arm, trying to break her father's grip and accidently smacking Bobby in the face as he sat next to her in the car. Her face was wet with tears and her body shaking.

"Piper," Bobby said soothingly, trying to calm her limbs and wake her. "You're okay, it's just a dream."

She woke in a heat of self-consciousness and fear that hadn't yet subsided. She wiped her cheeks and felt every eye in the car staring at her. Betty used her hand to shoo away Jules' and Michael's stares from the front seat and, without a word, pulled Piper up against her. She smoothed her hair and let her rest her head on her shoulder. Bobby wanted to be comforting Piper right now, but Betty was in a better position. Piper was more open to her help, and Betty had years of maternal experience at scaring away the monsters that live in dreams.

When they finally pulled up to the address Chris had given them, they'd all but stopped speaking to each other. In need of a stretch, a shower, and some personal space, they spilled out of the car. It was the middle of the morning now, and the sun was nothing but an annoying reminder that they hadn't had a true night's sleep since before Jules was taken.

The house was cookie-cutter perfect, one of many in a row on a quiet cul-de-sac. Pale green with a white picket fence and dark shutters, it was what one would imagine suburban life to be. The bushes were perfectly squared, the walkway was free of any weeds, and the paint on the railings leading up the front stairs was sparkling white. This house looked more like it was dropped from the sky than built or maintained. It displayed a light blanket of snow, adding to its curb appeal. It lacked any flaws, but also any character.

Betty felt the cold air fill her lungs. "It's colder than a witch's belt buckle on the shady side of an iceberg out here. Someone should have warned me. My sweaters are going to need sweaters. This is the first time I've ever been outside of North Carolina." Turning toward Jules who was edging her way tentatively out of the car, favoring her injured leg, she said, "Your father and I honeymooned on the Blue Ridge Mountains. That's really the only vacation I've ever been on." She laughed a little. "Not that I'm calling this a vacation, it's just nice to see someplace new, even if it is freezing cold."

This struck everyone as depressing, though that wasn't Betty's intention. She loved her life with Stan, and before he was killed they had planned for plenty of traveling after he retired from the police force. "Don't look at me like I'm a dead dog, for goodness sake," she retorted, shaking her hands at their sorry-looking expressions. "You never know where life is gonna take you, I've got no regrets so far."

As they unloaded their bags from the trunk, Chris stepped out the front door and casually strode down the steps toward them.

"You all look like hell," he said, extending his hand to Bobby. "Hopefully I can make you comfortable here. We've just gotten settled in ourselves, so you'll have to bear with us."

"We're just grateful for the help, Chris. I'm sorry to spring this on you. I'm sure you didn't think you'd be hearing from me quite so soon," Bobby said, throwing a bag over his shoulder. "This here is my friend Betty Grafton, her daughter, Jules, and this is Piper." He struggled to label Piper. Was she his girlfriend? His ex? The love of his life? He really didn't know right now. "You already know Michael very well." Whether it was meant to sound like it or not, that last statement cut a little. Michael got the hint, chatting with Christian after he'd been relocated was against the rules and Bobby wasn't pleased.

"Well, my son is going to sleep on a cot in my room. That leaves two other bedrooms and a pullout couch in the office. I'll let you all fight it out."

Betty cut in quickly, barely hiding her ulterior motive. "I'll take the pullout in the office. Jules and Michael, you take one bedroom. Let's get on in the house and brush the stink off of us. I'm more stir crazy than a caged canary." No, she hadn't told Piper and Bobby to bunk up together, she hadn't called them out, but in her masterful way she had implied it.

Bobby and Piper looked at each other, he with a grin, she with a scowl. "I hope you like the floor," she said, shoving another bag into his chest and following the group into the house.

Michael let out a little howl of laughter as he crouched for Jules to put her arm over his shoulder. Her leg was still too tender to walk on fully, and she loved leaning on him. Literally and figuratively, he was solid. They hadn't had a chance to talk more about what happened between them, but all of his actions were speaking for him now. He had decided to come even when he didn't have to. They'd need to sort it all out at some point, but right now that was enough for her.

As they entered the house, they saw its interior was as nondescript as its exterior. The paint was fresh, the trim all beveled and detailed beautifully. It was a perfectly polished space, pulled from the pages of a magazine. It was staged to be a home where you could just show up and start your life rather than one you'd been creating for years.

Betty, in her usual commanding way, made herself right at home, and home to her was in the kitchen. She assessed the room.

"What on God's green earth is all this?" Betty asked as she intrusively pulled open Chris's refrigerator. She was faced with boxes of takeout food and cans of soda. "There isn't a single vegetable in this house. Is this what you've been feeding your child? Don't you cook?"

"I'm still getting settled in as the assistant admissions consultant at the university. Actually, I'm still trying to figure out what the assistant admissions consultant is supposed to do every day. I haven't had a lot of time to go food shopping. Not that I'd know what to do with the food anyway. The closest thing I do to home cooking is occasionally use my nonna's cookbook as a coaster," Chris said smiling. Betty was a refreshing reminder of the women of his mother's generation.

"You have your grandmother's cookbook? Oh, stop my beating heart! I know people who would pay a pretty penny for her baked beans recipe. I remember fights nearly breaking out at bridge tables over who would get to take home her leftovers. She was an amazing cook and a peach of a woman."

"You knew my nonna?" Christian asked, taken aback by the connection. He wasn't allowed to take much when he hastily left Edenville, but the cookbook, his last connection to his grandmother, had made the cut. There was no one in the world who had loved him more unconditionally than his father's mother. Well, as a child anyway. As he got older and made questionable decisions, her fondness for him seemed to dwindle. When she grew close to death, when cancer was about to take her, he was too caught up in impressing his father to even visit her. It was one of his biggest regrets.

"Only a casual acquaintance, but I sure remember her talking about you. She thought you walked on water. I remember my aunt bringing her flowers when she was moved to hospice care, and she said she talked about you the whole time. She was a very special woman. May I take a peek at that book? It's like the Holy Grail of Edenville, people still talk about her recipes."

Chris fought the urge to ask for more details. He doubted there would be anything she could tell him that would heal that old wound. "Sure." He crossed his living room and pulled an old, light blue book from a shelf. "Knock yourself out," he said, shocked by the joy spreading across Betty's face.

She pulled the book onto her lap and started flipping the pages at a frantic pace. As the group returned to their casual conversation about the area attractions and the Midwest weather, they all jumped, startled when Betty hopped to her feet and shouted, "Nutmeg! I can't have y'all eating takeout when we have this amazing book of recipes here. Where's the closest market?"

Chris scanned the room with a look that questioned, *Is she serious?* The wide grins he was met with let him know she did indeed mean business.

"Let's go, Betty," Chris said, grabbing his keys off the counter. "If you can make my nonna's zabaglione, I'll pick you up an engagement ring while we're out."

Chapter Thirteen

EVERYONE WAS MORE than ready for bed by ten that night. Each was exhausted from the day and full from the meal Betty had cooked. It had been a veritable feast of pasta fagioli, lasagna, and cannoli. Betty had spent the entire afternoon toiling away, filling the house with amazing smells. Little Chris had perched himself on the stool at the kitchen counter and watched her intently, asking a litany of questions that mostly began with *why*. They ranged from "Why are you here?" to "Why is that pot making that noise?" Some people may have been annoyed by his persistence, but every time Big Chris came to check on her tolerance level, Betty would shoo him away.

She missed having a set of eyes fixed on her as she cooked. She missed what it meant to set an example for someone. All her people were grown now, and sure, she gave them advice at times, but none of them looked at her with such interest and admiration as Little Chris was now. She loved seeing the wonderment on his face as he tried to understand how she knew how to grease a baking dish and fill a frosting bag. At that age, the things she was doing in the kitchen were as entertaining and impressive as magic tricks, and she loved an audience.

Now that the meal was over, the dishes clean, and the house quiet, Piper was restless. She crept through the house and out the front door, settling onto one of the cushioned wicker porch chairs. It wasn't quite the escape she'd found on the swing at Betty's, but it would have to do. She didn't want to step over Bobby on her way to bed and have to lie there awake, fighting every urge to speak to him. She'd hide out here until it was late enough to assume Bobby was asleep. The porch was screened but the air was freezing, and she was grateful for the soft throw blanket hanging on the back of her chair. She draped it over her and pulled her knees up, curling herself up for warmth.

She was shocked when out stepped Chris, two empty glasses and a bottle of amber alcohol in his hand. After her run-in with his brother, Sean, it would be expected that she'd never want to share a drink with another Donavan. But hey he wasn't really a Donavan anymore was he? Her mind should have been filled with anxiety about sitting alone on the porch with a man who'd done some very criminal things in his life. But Piper had watched him that day back in the warehouse, the day he'd almost killed the judge. She watched him wrestle with the evil inside him and beat it back. That, paired with the way he clearly adored his son, was enough to put her at ease. No one could have that type of tenderness for a child and also be a danger to her. She had the unfortunate experience of staring into the eyes of wickedness, and Chris's weren't that kind of dangerous. They were smoldering, the kind of eyes that would compel a woman to make terrible choices just for the chance to look into them one more time. He wasn't at all her type, but she could see how a woman would throw caution to the wind and roll the dice on a guy like Chris.

He sat in the chair next to her and placed the glasses and bottle on the table between them. "I guess I owe you an apology. I didn't realize what happened between you and my brother. Bobby gave me the gory details. So on behalf of my family, I'm sorry." Chris tipped the bottle of bourbon into the stout glass tumblers and slid one over to Piper.

"He's lucky to have you," Piper smiled, intentionally not accepting his apology. She was glad Sean was seeking treatment, but she wasn't ready to forgive him.

"As a peace offering I'd like to extend an invitation to you. It's for a very exclusive club that few people qualify for. It's called *The I'm the Child of a Monster Club,* and you've made the cut. Actually, judging by your story, you could be the president." Chris smirked and reached his glass over toward hers, clanking them together in mock celebration. "Welcome, now you get to ask me questions about how to muddle through life when no one has showed you how."

Piper took a minuscule sip of the alcohol and cringed as the heat burned its way down her throat. She hadn't really thought how much she and Chris may have in common, but he was right. She found herself suddenly very curious about Chris's life, so if he was opening that door, she was going to walk through it. She put her glass back on the table and prayed she wouldn't need to toast again. "I do have a question for you. When your dad died, how did it feel?" She didn't frame the question to lead him to an answer; she wanted honesty.

Chris paused, then tilted his head back and filled his mouth with the final sip of his bourbon. As he swallowed it he cleared his throat, ready to give her what he had promised.

"If you're asking if I missed him, if I mourned him, no. How did I feel? For the first time in my adult life I felt free, like the idea of this," he waved his hands around him at the house, the suburban street, "could all be possible someday. As long as my father was alive I was trapped, Sean was trapped, and it wouldn't be long before my son was, too. But the second he died, we were free. It took years more before we could find the right path out, but now, we're finally here. We have a chance for a normal life. Now my question for you, if you were faced with the opportunity tomorrow, would you kill your father?" Chris tipped the bottle again and filled his glass.

It was a loaded question and one that gave her pause. She'd love to say she'd never envisioned killing her father, but that wasn't the case. She feared that was the part of him inside her, the one that could fantasize about rising against him and gladly taking his life. But those were just dreams. "If he were trying to kill me or hurt someone else, I would kill him. But if putting him in prison was an option, I would think I'd be fine with that." Judging by Chris's face, she could tell he didn't agree.

"Until there isn't any breath left in his lungs, until his heart pumps its last beat, you won't find any peace. You may think you will, but when you get your first letter from prison, or when your child asks where your father is, you'll realize he's still haunting you." Chris took another sip of his drink and tightened his lips over his teeth as it ran down his throat.

"Are you saying, given the chance, you'd have killed your father?" Piper took another swig of her drink as well. This time she couldn't keep from wincing, but she was starting to understand why people drank this stuff. It burned like hell, but the burn was followed by a whole-body warming and a soothing feeling. It was a nice contrast to the frigid night air.

Chris's eyes flashed with a ghostly memory, and in a low voice replied, "Who said I didn't?" The moment hung between them like the silence of the night. This wasn't the kind of talk you could have with *normal* people. This wasn't dinner conversation, but she actually found it refreshing to connect to someone on this level. Bobby may have loved her, but she couldn't say he understood her, or she him.

After she watched Chris throw back the rest of his drink, Piper found the words she was looking for. "I'm not sure I could kill him if I was given the chance. I don't know if I have that in me. But I wouldn't cry if it happened, that's for sure. Could I do it myself? I don't think so."

"You'd be amazed what you're capable of when you are faced with something so evil."

She shrugged her shoulder and asked another question. "Now that you're here and you have your fresh start, do you feel different? Do you feel fixed?" Piper was hoping she'd hear a resounding *yes*—that he'd declare himself whole and warm and fuzzy, but she knew that wasn't likely.

Chris pondered the question. It was more complicated than just a quick yes or no. He wanted to be realistic but optimistic. He knew she wasn't asking because she cared how he was doing. She wanted to hear if there was hope for her. He wanted to give her that hope. "Sydney Collingsworth. She's my boss, and I hate her," he said, crossing his legs and lounging back in his chair. He didn't really hate her, she just annoyed him, and he didn't like the way she made him feel. "She's a real uptight prude. She thinks I'm a moron and that I don't deserve to work at the university, and she's probably right. But my point is, that's my biggest problem right now. I'm not meeting with any drug lords to strike a bargain to keep my friends alive. I am not sitting in handcuffs. I'm pissed because my boss, some neurotic little blonde with legs that go on forever, is treating me like crap.

"I still look over my shoulder. I still can't really connect with people, but on a day-to-day basis my life, my son's life, is better. It took time, it wasn't like my father was gone and I immediately knew what to do with myself, but it was the first step. Now, why you are sitting out on my porch when there's a guy in there who seems to care a lot about you?"

Piper had a feeling he'd bring this up. The tension between her and Bobby was not something she had been trying to hide. On the contrary, she'd been pouring salt in that wound any time the chance arose. It was how she kept from kissing him; it's how she kept her hands off of him, by constantly reminding herself why she was upset. "It's complicated. Bobby and I are just too different. He's a cop first, and that doesn't exactly work with everything I have going on. He betrayed me when I needed him the most."

"And then he got in the car and drove halfway across the country to make sure you're safe. I think you have to remember, Piper, this stuff is part of your normal life, but that's not the case for everyone else. You can't expect Bobby to board your crazy train and then just become the conductor. There's a learning curve to living this kind of life. My wife couldn't deal with it, and I let her go. If I'd made the choice earlier to walk away from that life I'd still have her. Maybe cut him some slack. Actually, forget the maybe, get off my porch and go swallow your pride. In my experience, if you have people willing to look past all your baggage, don't walk away from them. Trust me, there won't be people lining up to take their place."

Piper drew in a long breath, took the last mouthful of her

bourbon, and choked it down painfully.

"How in the world do you drink this garbage?" she asked, her face twisted in disgust. She stood up and walked toward the door, patting his shoulder as she passed.

"It can't taste worse than the crow you're about to eat," he joked, tipping the bottle into his cup and filling it again.

Piper quietly made her way through the dark house, trying to ignore the voice in her head that was telling her nothing would ever work between her and Bobby, that making amends was prolonging inevitable heartbreak.

As she pulled open the bedroom door, she saw Bobby lying on the floor in a twisted position that had to be painfully uncomfortable. It was no wonder he was still wide awake.

"Get off the floor," Piper murmured. She stepped over him and pulled her sweater over her head, leaving her in just her white tank top. Bobby shot up, looking confused.

"What's the matter?" he asked, immediately assuming something had gone wrong.

"Well, my father's a serial killer determined to kill me, I've never in my life had a decent relationship with anyone, I don't know how to make things work, and I don't know how to be in love. So, that's what's wrong. I'm wrong. So get off the floor, get in bed, and hold me while I try to figure out how to be with you."

Bobby sat stunned, her words taking time to sink in. He assumed an apology would be something he'd be giving. He figured they had miles more to go, hours more to talk before they could come to any place of peace between them.

"You don't have to apologize to me, Piper. I'm the one who should be saying that I'm sorry. I completely blindsided you that day. I don't know how we'll make it through all this, but I know I want to try. I want to try to be with you." He stood, stretched his sore back, and stepped toward her, still hesitant.

Piper unbuttoned her jeans and slid them down her body. She reached back and unhooked her bra, slipped herself out of it and pulled back the blankets of the bed. She slid in and exhaled as the weight of her anger left her. "Bobby, shut up. Get in bed."

He smiled widely and pulled his shirt over his head. Joining her between the sheets was like coming home. Before this, they had only had a taste of each other and then fallen apart, split by the differences between them. That time away had made them desperate for one another, and the hunger they had now was evident. It showed in every slide of his hand and every seductive moan in her throat.

There was no hesitation this time, no joking around. Not an awkward moment. Bobby didn't gently peel away the remainder of her clothes; he tore at them, eager to have her skin against his. His desperation made every touch excite her more. He was almost frantic in his need to have her, and it was thrilling to be wanted so badly, needed so urgently. It was as if kissing her neck or the motion of forcefully pulling her body onto his was the medicine he needed to survive. She gave herself to him fully, her body was his to own—and he took that responsibility seriously. This was not just about pleasing her—this was about possessing her.

The fierceness in his eyes didn't frighten Piper; it brought her even closer to the edge of ecstasy. She had told him, *you can have me*—and he wasted no time on consequences or risks. His sheer lack of hesitation was as sexy to Piper as the pulsing of his bicep or the carved chest muscles she was currently caressing.

He rolled her onto her back, gazing over her body like a man who'd seen heaven. He stroked his warm hands up her smooth and trembling legs and separated them. His body covered hers and she wrapped her arms around him, dragging him down to her, into her. She trailed her nails down his back as he buried his face in her neck. This is what make-up sex should be.

113

Chapter Fourteen

THE NEXT TWO weeks were oddly comfortable for Chris. He had taken warmly to the noise in his house. He was overjoyed by the sincere connection that had grown between Betty and his son. She had cooked and baked her way almost completely through his nonna's recipe book. He'd gained six pounds, but the memories that flooded back with every bite made his snug jeans well worth it.

The rest of the group, however, was growing restless. They'd been away from their jobs, their routines, and their friends for long enough. They were missing their lives. Only Michael and Bobby had told their bosses about their need for time off. Michael claimed a family emergency while Bobby said he needed some space from all the reporters hunting him down as a source. He'd saved up several weeks of vacation, never wanting to be the guy who missed anything at work. Captain Baines was still flying high from the praise he was receiving due to his department's *forward thinking* and *initiative*, as it was being called from the higher-ups. He couldn't care less if Bobby was gone for the year. As a matter of fact, Bobby's absence meant it was less likely that he'd be there to collect any accolades for contacting the FBI and linking the cases. More attention for Baines.

Jules and Betty hadn't told anyone they were leaving. That was a strategic choice. Leaving quickly without anyone knowing meant less likelihood of being followed—or hunted, as the case may be. Now, however, as time ticked by they worried about their jobs and felt guilty for leaving their friends without a word. Would they have lives to walk back into? They'd all left their phones behind, knowing they could be traced. They bought burn phones to keep in touch with each other, but the disconnected feeling was starting to box them all in.

Bobby had been monitoring the news back in Edenville and the more he watched the more he realized leaving was the right answer. The town had become a media zoo. The residents were up in arms about the extra attention and the danger lurking in their midst. They were looking for someone to blame. That was all reason enough to be glad for the break in Illinois, but he knew staying here wasn't a permanent solution. He knew Piper would want to face this head on at some point, and she'd need him to stand by her, not stand in her way.

To ease the claustrophobic feeling, Piper and Bobby walked through Chris's quiet neighborhood trying to fill the purposeless day. It was cold here, a type of cold Bobby barely remembered from his childhood. They'd both borrowed extra coats from Chris, and Bobby couldn't get over how small Piper looked in the much-too-big jacket. She had forgotten how much she missed the crunching of snow under her feet. It was a nice thing to hear again.

"I've been giving this a lot of thought," Piper said, hoping Bobby would be open to her idea. "I think we should check in with Agent Carlson. We don't need to tell her where we are. I'd just like to know where they are in the case."

Bobby had committed himself to *trying*. He'd try opening his mind and closing his mouth. He knew there would still be moments that he'd have to speak up, but small concessions like this were a good place to start. Making love to her and making up with her had filled him with the willpower to attempt to find middle ground. He pulled his new phone from his pocket and handed it to her. "I agree," he said quietly, "just keep it short."

"Really?" she asked, stunned by his quick support. She snatched the phone before he could reconsider.

"Don't look so surprised that I finally think one of your ideas isn't terrible. There's a first time for everything." He put his arm around her as she dialed. He heard the phone connect and knew immediately by the look of confusion on Piper's face that something wasn't right.

"Is Agent Carlson there?" she hesitantly asked the male voice that answered her call.

"Is this Piper?" the man asked in an all business manner.

"Who is this?" Piper shot back, ready to disconnect the phone if she didn't like the answer.

"This is Agent Carlson's supervisor, Special Agent Miles Stanley. She's been missing for over a week. Once you went off the radar she went hard into finding you and your friends. Then last week she dropped her badge, gun, and phone at the police precinct here and hasn't been heard from since. We weren't sure if you'd taken off on your own or if it was foul play. Can you confirm that you left under your own volition and are under no duress?" The man spoke robotically, unemotionally.

"I'm fine. After my friend Jules was attacked we didn't feel safe in Edenville anymore. We made the decision to leave. Are you thinking that Agent Carlson is in some kind of danger? Do you think my father is involved?"

"We don't have any leads right now. The last footage we have of her doesn't suggest any foul play. This case has been really hard on her over the years. Once you went missing I think she may have needed to take a step back. I'm worried about her, but I know she can take care of herself out there. Piper, I need to ask you to come back to Edenville. You are the closest person to this case. I know Agent Carlson can be abrasive. Her tactics seem insensitive at times. I'd like to take a different approach. If you're willing, I'd like you to sit down with our profiling team. No one knows your father and his history better than you. He's a creature of habit and rituals. You are our greatest source in finding out where he is and what he does next."

"I understand, Agent Stanley. I need some time to think about it. Can I call you back in a little while?" Piper had stopped walking, unable to move her legs and think straight at the same time.

"Of course," Agent Stanley said. "I don't make this request lightly. I know how dangerous and troubling all this is. I can assure you, you'll have the full support and protection of my team. I know your interactions with us up to this point have been turbulent, but that won't be the case when you come back. We want to capture your father and ensure our agent's safety, but we need your help to do that."

Piper thanked him for his time and hung up the phone. Bobby, who had waited patiently throughout the phone call, was now standing in front of Piper, eyes wide with anticipation.

"I need to go back," she whispered, looking past him. "Please come with me?" She stepped forward and he opened his arms to her. He patted down the fluttering pieces of her hair and spoke reassuringly.

"I'll go back with you," Bobby said. "Speaking of going back, do you think it's safe to go back to Chris's? I just realized we left Michael and Jules alone. That's something I don't want to walk in on."

The house was quiet. Piper and Bobby had stepped out; Betty had gone with Chris and his son into town for more groceries. The opportunity was right, Jules thought, but was she ready?

"How's your leg feeling?" Michael asked as he came up behind Jules and wrapped his arms around her. Even though she knew it was him, even though she knew he was about to touch her, she still jumped.

Jules hadn't felt safe in her own skin since the day of her abduction. It didn't matter how many miles were between her and Edenville now, she still couldn't stop seeing the killer's face. She had spent mere moments with the monster, but he had left his haunting mark forever etched into her leg. She could only imagine what a lifetime with him must have done to Piper.

"The leg is doing much better, the jumpiness, I'm afraid, hasn't really subsided." She turned her body around, nestling

117

into his massive chest. She may not feel completely safe anywhere, but the closest she came to it was in Michael's arms.

"It'll get better, I promise." He leaned down and kissed her. They hadn't made love since their argument, before she was taken. Their bodies were hungry for each other, but she knew he wouldn't push her. If and when she was ready for him, she'd need to initiate it. The scent of his cologne and the feel of his body pressed up against hers, made her think maybe she was ready. Yes, she decided, feeling her body respond with desire, it's time. She tore her lips from his and nibbled lightly on his ear. He moaned a primal groan, and embraced her tighter. She could feel his longing and responded with a sweet purr of her own. It was clear now—permission granted.

There were times Jules felt nervous about her ability to please Michael. He was such a skilled lover and had been able to bring her to places she'd never experienced before—over and over again. He never seemed to tire of exploring her body, treating her ecstasy like a challenge and never wanting to give anything less than every ounce of energy he had. Now as they crossed the room, clothes peeling away, he bent to lift her onto the bed and she winced in pain as her leg moved too quickly.

"I'm sorry," he said, lowering her back to the ground. "I forgot." The fear in his eyes that he had hurt her endeared him to Jules even more. They had yet to sort out what they were as a couple, but there was no doubting who he was as a man. She smiled up at him and ran her hand over his unshaven face calming his worry about her pain. She lay on the bed and tugged him down on top of her. "I'm not going to break," she whispered seductively into his ear. "Though if you play your cards right I might scream." She ran her nails, pressed firmly into his skin, up his back and he shuddered with anticipation. She had learned during their many encounters what it took to make his eyes close and his body tremble. He was a man who loved the sensation of nails on his skin, the harder the better. When he danced his finger over her lips she'd lick it seductively and he'd nearly lose his mind.

He'd mastered the same roadmap to her body as well. She'd grab tightly at the sheets and arch her back any time he softly bit down on her skin, just a nibble would send her into a frenzy, something she hadn't known about herself until she met Michael. His amazing tongue and fluttering fingers roaming her body had liberated her from the mediocre lovemaking she'd assumed was as good as it got.

Now with Michael, as he found another spot to lightly sink his teeth into, she realized this was the way it was meant to be. Each time should exceed the last. Both of them should be writhing with pleasure, and she could tell already this encounter would live up to that standard.

Chapter Fifteen

"I'M NOT SURE about this." Betty frowned as she packed up a cooler full of homemade food for their car ride back. "Are you two sure you should go back? Maybe Michael should go with you, just for an extra set of eyes."

"I think it's better if Piper and I go back on our own. It sounds like Agent Carlson's disappearance has taken everything up a notch. I don't doubt that we'll get all the protection we need. They really want to work with Piper to see what pertinent information she might have that could help them determine her father's next move. Agent Carlson always seemed to discount Piper's ability to help, whereas Agent Stanley seems anxious for it."

Chris stood blocking his front door, arms folded across his chest. "I'm not a fan of this at all. Of course the FBI wants you back in town, you're bait. Do you really think they want to protect you more than they want to attach their names to the takedown of a notorious killer? I think you should stay."

Piper had considered all of these angles as well. She knew there was a great risk, but she didn't feel like she had many viable options. Even if Chris enjoyed the company, housing five people who had recently abandoned their jobs and lives was probably less appealing long term.

"You're just afraid we'll put all this to bed and you'll lose Betty cooking all your childhood favorites," Piper quipped, knowing his sentiment was nice but that her mind was already made up.

"Maybe," he said, winking over at Betty. He moved away from the door and shook Bobby's hand. As Piper approached him, she felt an odd sense of sadness. She hadn't really thought about the fact that, after today, it was unlikely they'd connect with Chris again. He'd need to limit his communication with anyone in Edenville, and his debt had more than been paid. This brief vacation from reality was coming to a close. Chris opened his arms to her for a hug, clearly understanding the finality of this moment. Piper had been a kindred spirit to him.

Someone who could look at him and not see everything he lacked, but understand everything that made him tick. She leaned into his hug, squeezing him the way Betty had done for her, the way Betty had taught her. He spoke quietly into her ear. "You've got a long ride back, make sure you get right with what you're willing to do. Remember what I told you. As long as he's living, he'll haunt you."

She had remembered his words. They'd been swirling around in her head since he had said them. And she continued to ask herself, again and again, whether she'd be able to kill her father, given the chance. She still didn't have the answer.

The ride back toward North Carolina had long, stretching moments of silence. Not an awkward silence that made her squirm in her chair and search for words, but a comfortable quiet that gave them both time to run through the gamut of emotions they were feeling. Joy to have made amends. Sadness to be leaving somewhere they found some comfort. Fear for what might be to come.

"I don't think we'll be able to drive straight through. We're just about to cross over into West Virginia. Why don't we stop for the night?" Bobby suggested as he stretched his back and moaned with discomfort. Piper was anxious to get back, but she also didn't mind one more night with Bobby in a place she felt safe, a place she could still be anonymous.

They pulled into the parking lot of a tiny motel with a blue flashing vacancy sign. Bobby ran into the office and emerged with a room key and a bottle of something Piper couldn't make out.

"What is that?" she asked, gesturing at the bottle as she followed Bobby to the door of their room.

"This is the finest seven dollar bottle of champagne the Motel Crimson Moon has to offer." He turned the key in the door and pushed his shoulder into it.

"Are we celebrating something?" Piper asked as she stepped hesitantly into the dated musty room. The carpet was thick orange shag and the curtains looked like they hadn't been updated in decades. "Maybe we should save the bottle and if we wake up tomorrow without bed bugs we'll toast to that miracle."

"It's not so bad," Bobby grinned dropping his bag and pulling Piper in close to him. "I'm sure we can make the best of it." He leaned down and kissed her neck sending her into a frantic giggle. Spinning around, he released her and she flopped herself on to the bed.

"I'm saving this bottle," he whispered as he lay down beside her, tucking her hair back behind her ear. "We're going to open this when we're all back together in Edenville. When your father is in prison and you're safe, we'll pop this cork start our lives together."

The lights in the room flickered and then with a pop, went out completely. Piper closed the space between herself and Bobby with a leap in his direction. The thudding of her heart was all she could hear now that the humming of the heater had ceased. "What was that?" she asked, digging her nails slightly into his bicep.

"I don't know what caused it, but I sure like the effect." He took her hand and pulled it to his lips for a kiss. "There aren't very many things you can do in the dark, we'll have to make our own entertainment." He kissed her fingertips one by one, then her palm, her wrist, all the way down the soft skin of her arm to her elbow.

"Hide and seek?" she teased. "Flashlight tag?" she slipped her free hand under the front of his shirt and caressed his tight stomach, then ran her hands over the buckle of his belt.

"I'd kick your ass in flashlight tag." Bobby tickled her, fingers dancing up her spine.

Piper wiggled away and as his fingers turned from teasing to tantalizing she leaned into his lips and kissed him. She never wanted this to stop feeling so powerful, combustible. The fear of her father was tangible, very real, but the fear of one day waking up and not feeling the magnetically fierce attraction to Bobby was a different kind of frightening.

She broke the kiss but kept her face close to his, their noses almost touching. The dark room came alive once more as the lights crackled and hummed back on all at once. They stared at each other, eyes locked together.

"I'm scared," Piper whispered, taking in a deep breath and holding it. When Bobby's warm hand brushed her cheek she released it, letting the tightness in her chest subside for a moment.

"He isn't going to hurt you," Bobby assured her, his hand firmly grasping hers.

"I'm not just afraid of him. I'm scared of anything that stops me from being able to feel like this, anything that would take me away from having this kind of moment every day. There aren't too many perks to never being in love, but one of them is that you don't know what you're missing. I never want to live without this, without you."

"You won't," Bobby said definitively. He had learned during his training that you never make a promise, especially when you can't completely control the outcome. But how do you look in the face of the woman you love, listen to her ask you for something, and not give it to her? Piper needed a promise, she needed to be assured, and just like he'd give her his last drink of water if they were stranded in the desert, he'd give her this.

They didn't make love. She curled tighter into his arms, and though the spark of their passion was ignited, her jagged nerves needed something different tonight. One of the best things about Bobby was that she didn't need to speak for him to be able to see that. He kissed her forehead lightly and smoothed her hair back away from her face. He'd hold her all night if that was what it took to make her feel safe.

The next morning's drive felt like a miserable chore. Neither of them wanted to get in the car and face what lay ahead of them. The hotel may have been an outdated dump but it was a place they could be alone together, safe. Piper was sorry to have to leave. It was just past lunchtime as they drove past the "Welcome to Edenville" sign, and Piper heard the funny jingling ring of Bobby's unfamiliar new phone.

"Is it Michael again? We told him we'd check in every two hours, and we have. He needs to relax."

"It isn't him. It's a blocked number." Bobby put the phone to his ear and answered with a skeptical hello.

"Bobby?" Agent Carlson asked in a weary voice. "I heard through the grapevine that you and Piper agreed to come back to Edenville. I need to meet with you both."

Bobby assumed that grapevine was not made up of casual conversations with her colleagues but more likely the questionable use of FBI technology to listen in on phone conversations and find phone numbers. Leaving her phone behind at the precinct was probably a strategic move. He guessed it had been linked to another phone or device she was using to stay connected to the case.

Bobby didn't bother heading down that path, she wouldn't tell him how she'd gotten his new number anyway, so why waste the breath. "We're planning to meet with Agent Stanley when we get back to town. He led us to believe you weren't easy to get a hold of at the moment. Maybe you'd gone a little rouge agent or something."

"Frankly, I have. I need to meet with you both before I go back in to see my superiors. There are things you need to hear directly from me, and once I speak with them, I doubt I'll have my chance to meet with you again. Please, I'm at Saint Julian's Church. I'm begging you. I only need a few minutes."

"Carlson," Bobby said, his voice full of skepticism, "if you were in our position, would you consider meeting under these circumstances?"

"If you were in my position, you'd realize you had no other

choice. This isn't a trap, no hidden agenda. I have something to tell you. I just need you to hear me out. Please, come to the church. I have something to give Piper." This wasn't the brash, egotistical person Bobby had dealt with on every previous occasion. Her voice was cracking with exhaustion. She sounded desperate.

"We'll be there in twenty minutes. But we aren't hanging around long. Let's keep this meeting right on the street, in a crowded public place."

As Bobby recounted the conversation to Piper he tried to emphasize the strain in Carlson's voice, the difference he heard, and the reason he'd agreed to meet her.

"I think you're right Bobby, I think we should go. You'd better call Michael. It's just about that time again."

"Let's wait until after we meet with Carlson, I don't want them all sitting there wondering what's going down. We'll fill them in after we hear what she has to say." The ride to Saint Julian's Church was a familiar one for Bobby. This was where he'd been confirmed, where he'd sat and listened to endless homilies, where he'd teased Betty for singing off-key. This was his church, though he'd been away from it for some time now. As they pulled up, his eyes were drawn to the familiar stained-glass window he'd always loved. It portrayed Saint Notker Balbulus, the patron saint of children who struggled to speak. It was donated by a wealthy parishioner whose son stuttered. Bobby sometimes spent the full hour of mass staring up at the glowing colors of the window.

"There she is," Piper said, pointing out the car window to Agent Carlson who was sitting solemnly on the large cement stairs of the church.

"Let's make sure we do this right, Piper. Be sharp, keep your eye out for anything that looks like a trap, and we'll keep it short." They exited the car, and Bobby surveyed the scene. There were plenty of people passing by on foot and in cars; lots of witnesses, making him feel slightly more secure.

Agent Carlson didn't stand as they walked up to meet her.

She remained seated on the cold stairs and looked down at her feet. "Thank you for coming," she murmured. "I wanted you to hear this from me first." She finally lifted her head and locked eyes with Piper. "Two years ago I was diagnosed with ALS. I was pissed. As a matter of fact, it was no more than a month before I met you, Piper. I had a few symptoms at the time, some muscle cramping and numbness in my arm, but I could mostly ignore them. Unfortunately, a couple of months ago, it got too big to ignore. My right arm has become so impacted that I can barely shoot my weapon any more. I can't continue to hide it."

"Why are you telling me this?" Piper asked, unsure of where this conversation was heading.

"I'm hoping that knowing this will give you the slightest bit of empathy for what I have to tell you. I'm hoping if you can't forgive me, you can at least try to understand my motivation. ALS is degenerative and aggressive. Best case, I have a few more months before I lose the ability to control my arm and then the muscle will atrophy. The doctors tell me the rest of my body will follow suit. I'll be confined to a bed. I'll be a prisoner, and the only hope I will have is that at some point my respiratory system will shut down and release me from my hell. There is no cure, nothing they can do for me. When the symptoms started to take over, I got desperate. I'd given my whole life to this job, and I'd devoted more than a decade to finding your father. The trail had grown completely cold, and when the profilers suggested that was because you were still alive, I had a revelation. Your father was as desperate to find you as I was to find him."

Her voice grew quiet and she dropped her gaze downward again. "I set up those two attacks on campus, and I leaked information about you to the media. I drew him here. I used you as bait. I just didn't want to die knowing he was still walking the streets. I want to live, even just for a little while, on a planet where he isn't free. When I leave here, I'm going to resign and tell them exactly what I've done. They'll bury this. I just wanted to be able to tell you myself."

126

As Piper opened her mouth to speak, a faint scream made its way to them from off in the distance. Bobby reached for his holstered weapon and looked down at Carlson, trying to read her expression. She seemed as stunned as they were about the noise. Then more screams, frantic hollering from just around the corner.

"Are you armed?" Bobby asked Carlson, knowing he'd have no choice but to find out what the commotion was. Carlson nodded yes and shakily rose to her feet while drawing her weapon.

Bobby looked at Piper, fighting with himself as the screams grew louder. "Stay here, stay with Agent Carlson." He ran off and rounded the corner of the church where a naked man stood swinging a hockey stick wildly. The crowd was scattering as Bobby read the scene. *What is this?* he wondered, *What is he doing? This seems like a—decoy.*

He saw two cruisers pull up to the scene and engage the man. Bobby turned on his heels and ran back toward the church. Then he heard it, the unmistakable popping of gunfire. He knew instantly that this was some kind of a set up and the odds of rounding the corner in time to save Piper were slim. This was where his training kicked in, it's what kept the fear from taking over, it kept the panic from slowing him down. He increased his speed by almost double, his gun gripped tightly in his hand. As he turned the corner he saw Agent Carlson down on the ground.

"Where is she?" he asked frantically, kneeling beside Carlson. He saw the other officers who had arrived at the scene of the naked man coming up behind him to assist.

"He drove off with her in a blue car, plate is C221BS. Heading west." Agent Carlson was gasping. "I got him in the shoulder I think. Take my car, it's faster than yours." She pushed her blood-covered keys into his hands, and he bolted for her car.

He crisscrossed the main streets of Edenville, flipping on Carlson's police scanner and tuning it to the local frequency. The information Carlson had given Bobby was already buzzing over the scanner—the plate number, the description of the car, and more importantly, the urgency of officer down, pursuit in progress. When a cop of any branch is shot, every badge on or off duty becomes part of the chase. In a small place like Edenville even retired officers grab their personal weapons and hit the streets.

Bobby sped quickly around each corner, not sure where he was headed, not clear what he was looking for, adrenaline pulsing through his veins. And then like a flash, a truck backing up too quickly from a driveway pulled in front of him. He slammed on his brakes, rubber grabbing for asphalt, but it was too late. Bobby felt the bursting of the airbag throwing him back in his seat as the car and truck collided violently. He was dazed as the driver of the truck ran to his window, trying to speak to him. Bobby squinted, blinked, and shook his head to try to refocus. The driver of the other vehicle stepped away, flagging down a passing police car.

When he finally got his bearings again, a familiar face was opening his car door. "Bobby, are you good?" Lindsey asked, seeming to appear out of nowhere.

"I'm fine," he said, taking a quick inventory of each of his limbs; all appeared to be uninjured.

"Let me call an ambulance. I've got to get back on the road, they're asking all available units to aid in the search."

"Can I ride with you?" he asked, desperate for any opportunity to help. "He's got Piper." Lindsey looked him over as he stepped out of the twisted car, making sure he wasn't injured.

"Let's go," she said, hustling back to her cruiser. As they started down the road they listened to the chatter on the scanner hoping someone had spotted the blue car by now. "Do you have any ideas where he would take her? They have the whole town pretty much on lockdown. He wouldn't have made it to any of the major highways, which have all been blocked off now. So if he were staying in Edenville, where should we look?"

"Nothing here means anything to him. We could clear a few

places like the spot they found Jules. Maybe Betty's house, Piper's apartment, but I can't imagine he'd head to any of those locations." His head was still foggy from the collision, and every scenario he ran through was more frightening than the last.

They drove to all the locations Bobby had mentioned, each turning up nothing. The sun had set now, and Bobby could feel his sadness filling the car. There was no way Piper was still alive, he thought. Her father was desperate to kill her. He'd have done it by now.

"Stop it," Lindsey barked, looking over at Bobby. "Stop letting yourself think about all that garbage and start thinking where else to look." He nodded his head, pushing back the tears starting to form and searched his mind for another idea.

Chapter Sixteen

"IT'S LIKE A family reunion," Piper's father mused, digging the gun into her ribs jestingly like he was tickling her rather than holding a deadly weapon. He swerved occasionally taking his hands off the wheel and his eyes off the road to taunt her. Piper felt herself growing numb. She didn't speak. She wouldn't give him the satisfaction of engaging him. She'd learned years ago that was what he wanted—a fight. "I've been looking for you." He pointed the gun at her again in a tsk-tsk kind of way. "You really screwed me up, you know. You were supposed to be dead. Don't you know you're number twenty-three? You can't go messing with something like that. I thought I'd lost you again, but I knew if I kept my eyes on that corrupt bitch who led me here in the first place, I'd find you. It's funny what a college student will do for twenty bucks. I mean, all I said was 'make a scene.' Who knew he'd be bare-assed and swinging a hockey stick?" He laughed manically, proud of himself and his superior intelligence.

"This is going to be so much fun." When they were far enough outside of the town, he hastily pulled off the road. Before Piper could react and try to escape the car, her father was upon her, gripping her wrists with his strong hands. She saw the zip ties he held between his teeth and understood his intention. She fought him, kept pulling her arms away, but with a swift thrust of his arm the butt of the gun made contact with the back of her head and her world went black. When she came to again her hands and feet were bound, and the sound of her father's voice was all she could hear. He was talking to himself in a way she recognized from her childhood. It was a monotone chant, something that seemed to focus him. As he saw her stir, he stopped speaking and gripped the steering wheel tighter. As she searched out the window for anything familiar, Piper started to realize they were heading toward the river, but she didn't recognize the exact route.

He switched the gun to his other hand and pulled out the small knife that he used to carve the number into her leg. He put the blade of the knife to her thigh and in one quick motion slit open her jeans, exposing the number carved into her leg. She didn't wince, she didn't move. She was stone. Whatever was about to come, she wouldn't give him the pleasure of emotionally partaking in it.

He looked down at her leg and his face filled with the pleasure one might get from seeing an old friend. This was the number that had lived, and after years of trying he was ready to right his wrong, correct his mistake—kill his daughter.

He continued to drive, speaking to her about all the things she didn't understand, trying to get her to realize how wrong her mother was, how evil and vindictive women can be, and why sometimes they just have to die. She ignored his words. She thought only of Agent Carlson, her arm shaking as she raised her weapon, too slow to avoid taking two shots to her stomach. She had gotten one shot off and it grazed his shoulder, but it took no more than a ripped shirt tied around it to stop the bleeding.

As she stared out the window, Piper finally saw something familiar. A small, carved sign in front of a tiny pink house read, *The Silter Family*, and Piper suddenly knew where they were going. This was the route to the cabin, the safe haven she'd escaped to while arguing with Bobby, that's where they were headed. Her father must have been following her, stalking her. He'd known the house was secluded and deserted. The idea of dying there actually brought Piper some peace. She'd think of Bobby, of Bruno. She'd hear the river rushing behind the house; she'd be okay with it.

When they pulled into the driveway of the cabin he pointed his gun in her direction again and glared at her with a warning.

"I'da killed you the last time you were here if it weren't for that damn beast of a dog you had with you." She remembered now her father's fear of dogs. It didn't really matter their size or their breed, any dog seemed to unsettle him. It was a memory she'd long forgotten until just now as she watched her father's face turn in disgust at the mention of Bruno. "Don't screw with me. Don't try anything. You know me—what I'm capable of. This can either be quick or I can drag it on, making you pray for death. You know that." And she did know that. She wasn't formulating a plan to escape right now. If the opportunity arose, she'd hit the alarm system. If she got the chance, she'd run. But she did know her father and what he could do to someone, and she wasn't going to make her move unless she was sure she could get away, because she couldn't deal with the punishment if she tried and failed.

He stepped out of the car and walked with purpose around to her side before yanking open the door and pulling her out by the arm. He lifted her and tossed her over his shoulder, carrying her like a sack of potatoes. He had always been a fit man, slimmed by his drug use but strong. Murder, the way he did it—up close and personal—required a certain strength and stamina.

A flash of memory filled Piper's mind. He had held her like this once before. She knew now it was after one of his murders when he had felt the sheer release and joy he got from killing. Margaret Oliver was a twenty-nine-year-old cocktail waitress who was attacked on her walk home from work. Her father had left the house the Wednesday night that Margaret was killed as a frantic, out-of-control man. That Friday he had returned home, radiating a calm that he obtained only from snuffing out someone's life. He had announced they would have an afternoon at the park. Piper was about seven years old, and for the first and only time in her life, she'd ridden the carousel. It felt like a fairy tale compared to her normal life—the whirling and the music were like an enchanted dream. She had felt at any moment her horse, painted pink and purple, would break free of the machine and they'd ride into the world together.

When the carousel stopped, her father reached out for her, and, smiling widely, tossed her over his shoulder and carried her halfway across the park, just as he was holding her now. They were both laughing, happy for the briefest of moments. No more than an hour after her carrousel ride, her father had set her on a park bench in one of the seediest neighborhoods in their city and went off to score some type of high. She'd waited alone on that bench for nearly two hours before she realized he'd probably forgotten about her. As the sun set that night, her little legs walked the two miles back to her apartment alone.

She didn't want to hold onto the memory of them laughing together, it was giving the man too much credit. It painted him in too bright a light. He laughed that day because he'd fulfilled his need to kill. He laughed because he'd taken away someone else's ability to ever laugh again. She carried the burden and guilt that came with knowing the only fond memories she had were grown from someone else's worst nightmare.

He dropped her off his shoulder and leaned her against the house as he opened the front door. Piper assumed the absence of any light and the lack of blaring alarms meant that her father had cut the power. As he pulled her into the house, it became clear he'd done more than that. He had staged the living room of the house, moved all the furniture to the walls and slid the large oak dining room table to the middle of the room. He'd planned this.

"Now we get to have some fun," he hissed as he dragged her across the room. She wasn't fighting him, wasn't clawing at the floor or pleading for her life. It wasn't because   she'd completely resigned herself to death, more that she understood her father's inner workings. She had a lifetime of watching him manipulate and control her mother. He knew exactly how to rile the woman and Piper would watch her father's growing pleasure as her mother fell further out of control. It was this ability to manipulate someone's reaction that brought him satisfaction. After she'd found out he was a serial killer she read every article she could find about him as well as information about other killers. At the time it calmed her to feel like she could turn his evil into something quantifiable, something you could cram into a medical journal rather than feel eating at your soul. She'd learned when her father felt like he was spiraling down the rabbit's hole, he saved himself by finding the ultimate place of control, determining if someone lived or died. When his victims begged for their lives it made him feel powerful, it filled that need to be superior. Staying silent would undermine that, and she was finding out quickly her plan was working.

"You aren't afraid?" he asked tauntingly, tapping the barrel of the gun to her cheek as he slammed her against the hard table. She didn't answer. "I guess I was right about you. You are like me, just like me." Piper looked away, fighting the urge to disagree with him. "Oh you don't think so? You're standing here about to die and you've got nothing to say. You know what normal people do? They cry, they all cry. They beg me to let them live. They *promise* they won't tell anyone. But not you, look at you," he shouted as he lifted her and slammed her down on her back with a thud on the oak table. He'd fastened ropes to the table legs and used them now to secure her to it. Flat on her back, unable to move, she readied herself for the pain to come. "You're just like me, you know this life is a joke, you know you'll never be one of those normal people with a happy life, so why bother? Why fight it? You're just like me," he repeated, clearly goading her on.

"Get it over with," she said through gritted teeth, turning her head away from him. She was staring out the sliding glass door now, gazing into the dark woods. She imagined Bruno out there, sniffing the air and lapping up water from the river.

"I will," he replied, angry at her stubbornness. "I'd better hurry up so I can get back to that redhead friend of yours. She's going to cry. As a matter of fact, she already did. She'll do a lot of begging, I can tell," he said with a glint in his eye.

"Go to hell!" Piper shouted, unable to ignore this jab. "You won't touch her. You'll never find her."

"People are stupid. They do stupid things because their

hearts tell them to." He let his face relax into one of mock pity and emotion. "Like come to your funeral, or visit your grave. They just can't resist it. I'll find her. As a matter of fact, even when you're dead, you'll lead me to her."

Piper finally fought against the ropes, furious and frightened at the idea. What if he was right? If she died, and Jules was next on his radar, there was a chance he could get to her. That thought was more terrifying than the sight of the large metal spike her father had just pulled from his pocket. He'd accomplished what he'd wanted. He'd made her fight back, made her want to live. Now he could take her life and start his evil over again. Finally, he'd be free to pick up where he'd left off.

He placed his gun down on a table next to the couch and took the small knife out again. Pulling open the slit in her jeans, he ran his fingers over the round, raised scar where he had previously plunged in the spike. He took a long look at the number he had carved two years ago. Smirking, he dug the blade into the healed wound and split it open again. She couldn't refrain from crying out, the pain was too great. She screamed as he continued to re-carve the number into her leg. His features were demonic, as though he were possessed by a malevolent power flowing into his body. The pleasure he was feeling from the pain he was inflicting was clear.

As he finished, Piper moaned, the agony burning its way through her leg, blood trickling onto the table. Physically it felt just as it had the first time, but emotionally she couldn't believe how different this attack was. She knew love and friendship now. She had lived. Yes, she wanted more time to enjoy what she'd just found, but at least she had found it. Maybe that was why she'd survived the first time, so she'd get a chance to have something real, something worth missing. She wasn't afraid to die, she only feared for what it would mean for those she was leaving behind.

"Finally," he groaned, looking like he was having an out-of-body experience. His eyes glassed over with evil. He yanked hard on the rope, tightening it. "You won't squirm this time. I won't miss again."

Chapter Seventeen

THE ONLY WAY to survive a life like his was to have incredible instincts, and luckily Chris did. They had carried him through dozens of near-death experiences, and he'd learned to trust his gut. This time, his gut feeling had him boarding a plane and heading for Edenville. He had tried to fight the nagging feeling, tried to convince himself that this wasn't his business. Eventually he couldn't ignore the voice in his head and he gave in to it. He wasn't about to let them walk into a trap or become pawns in a game to lure out a madman.

He'd need to be inconspicuous, a ghost, he thought as he rented a car at Raleigh-Durham International using one of his fake IDs. He couldn't walk the streets of his town or reach out to his friends. He was here for one reason, to quietly help if it was needed. It quickly became clear he'd made the right choice.

He'd packed a bag of things he thought he'd retired when he moved—a police scanner, a bulletproof vest, and an assortment of other items that might come in handy. Once he was settled in his rental car, a simple white sedan that was unlikely to draw any attention, he set up the scanner and heard it all play out. Officer down, woman abducted, Railway Killer. Blue car, gone. Finding them, he thought, would be difficult, maybe impossible, but if he did find them he'd need to be armed. The only place in Edenville he had dared to leave weapons was his cabin. The cabin none of his people, enemies or friends, had ever known about. It was his safe house. Not safe enough to harbor him indefinitely—he admitted he needed witness protection for that—but in a pinch he could hide there. It was a place to keep weapons, to keep information, and to keep his son if he ever needed to. He put his car in gear and started out for the cabin.

He'd go there first, arm himself, and then start his search for Piper. As he neared the cabin, he decided to park his car in a small clearing down the road and walk the rest of the way. He wanted to ensure it was safe, that no one from his old life had managed to connect the property to him. As he crept up the driveway he saw it. Like a lightning bolt of fate that he could only thank God for, the blue car was there, parked hastily and crooked in the driveway. How could this be? How could they be at his place?

Then it hit him. He had checked in with Michael three times since his relocation. He wanted to stay informed about the prosecutions and outcomes of many of his former employees and friends. It was technically against the rules, but hell, they'd all broken the rules leading up to this. So when he got the call weeks ago from Michael asking about a safe place for a client to stay for a short time, he immediately offered up the cabin. He had no use for it anymore, and the security measures he'd put in place had made it the perfect safe haven. Chris had been searching for ways to give back, good karma. It must have been for Piper, and her father must have been watching.

Chris quickly took cover in the trees surrounding the cabin. Slowly and carefully he made his way toward the house, keeping an ever-vigilant eye on the door and windows. When he was within ten yards of the cabin, he made a quick dash before shrinking himself down and sliding his back against the outer walls. Making his way around the side where he could see into the master bedroom, he peeked into the window and saw no movement. Suddenly he heard shouting coming from the other side of the house.

The lights were out; the alarm system keypad by the bedroom door was not blinking. The system had clearly been disabled. That meant the windows could be opened. He pushed the frame upward and breathed a sigh of relief as it slipped open quietly. It was the only thing standing between him and his gun, him and Piper.

He lifted himself through the window and rolled onto the

floor. He heard another scream, Piper howling in pain. He yanked open his closet door and pulled down the box from the top shelf. He loaded his Colt 45 and took in a deep breath. He had put himself in countless dangerous situations in his life, but rarely was he in a position of saving someone's life. The weight of this job was stifling; the thought of not getting to Piper in time was terrifying.

He stepped as lightly as he could though his room and towards the door that separated him from the commotion in the living room. As he reached for the knob his foot came down on a squeaky floorboard and he froze. Had it been heard over the yelling in the other room, had he given up the element of surprise? He gritted his teeth and decided either way this was the moment.

He flung open the door and took aim. As the man standing over Piper spun around to face him, surprised by the noise, Chris pulled the trigger. POP—the deafening noise seemed to shake the house.

Chapter Eighteen

BOBBY TAPPED HIS fingers anxiously on his leg as he and Lindsey pulled onto the main road. "We've cleared my place, Piper's place, Betty's house, and Michael's apartment. I can't think where else to check. Has there been any update over the radio?" Bobby's voice was both defeated and frantic. He'd counted every minute since Piper had been taken, and his math equaled up to the same thing—a man that desperate to kill would have done it already.

"Let's think this out," Lindsey said, trying to come up with a plan. "How long would he have been in Edenville prior to taking Piper? He took Jules, he made mention of them being friends. The news about the girls being attacked went national a few days prior to Jules's abduction. It wasn't linked to him on the news yet, but if he had been watching the updates about the attacks, maybe that was enough to draw him here. He had to have been watching Piper to know about her friendship with Jules. He would have staked out a place, planned this, just like he did when he took Jules. Something secluded, abandoned, off the beaten path." Bobby's face registered hope followed quickly by dread. His mind was racing faster than he could get the words out. "Piper and I were arguing, she was mad about the FBI. Michael put her up in the cabin—down by the river. If her father followed her, he'd have known it was empty..." Bobby trailed off, looking anxiously at Lindsey.

"Okay, that's where we head next," Lindsey responded in a steadying manner. She slapped Bobby on his shoulder, and he winced. It was still tender from the collision. She flipped on her cruiser lights and they wound through the streets making their way to the back roads leading to the river. It would take fifteen minutes, at least, and each passing moment felt like an eternity to Bobby. There was no guarantee they'd find Piper there, no promise that she'd be alive, but they had somewhere else to look, and that was enough for him right now.

Lindsey cut the lights and sirens when they were within a few miles of the cabin. Rounding the corner that led to the long dirt driveway, Bobby spotted a car parked slightly off the road—not the car that had been seen speeding away from the scene of Carlson's shoot out, but a white car with unfamiliar plates and a small sticker in the window that indicated it was a rental. Lindsey parked the cruiser then she and Bobby got out quickly. Seeing that the white car was empty, they moved toward the cabin on foot. There was the blue car. This was it. Their weapons were drawn as they crept cautiously, not disturbing the piles of leaves and sticks that would give away their position. Then they heard it, a single gunshot, and all attempts to be stealthy were over. Bobby ran forward at full speed as Lindsey grabbed the radio on her shoulder.

She read off the address of the cabin. "We have eyes on the car and shots fired. I repeat, we have shots fired. Requesting immediate backup to our location." Lindsey took off after Bobby, knowing procedure would have them wait, secure the perimeter and hold their position. But procedure meant little when love was involved.

Bobby kicked in the door and entered, his finger ready to squeeze the trigger with very little regard for who might be in his path. He felt Lindsey close behind him, and they both worked quickly to make sense of the scene.

"Chris?" Bobby stammered, loosening his trigger finger but not lowering his weapon. His brain could not connect the dots, something was not lining up here. Why was Chris standing here, his weapon pointed at a man doubled over on the ground as Piper lay tightly tied to the table, bleeding and in shock.

"Cut her loose," Chris ordered, his gun still pointed at Piper's father, his eyes locked on him. Lindsey shook off the confusion as she, too, tried to understand the scene. She pulled the utility knife from her belt and handed it to Bobby. "I have him covered, take care of Piper." Bobby was at her side in a flash and sawed at the ropes that were holding her down. She pushed against them, desperate to be off the table. There was sheer horror flashing in her eyes. Cutting these ties meant more than just freeing her from the danger in this room; it was releasing her from the constant fear of her father. It meant bringing her back to his side and never letting her go again. When the blade broke through the last fiber of rope, Piper rolled to her side and off the table, stifling sobs and breathing erratically. Bobby reached for her but she shook him off. Every ounce of strength she'd used to dam in her emotions was gone now, and they flooded her, nearly drowning her.

Bobby, assuming Piper was in shock, gave her room to breathe and turned his attention to Chris. He wanted to finish all of this quickly, end this reign of evil. "Chris, we got this now, lower your gun so Lindsey can search and cuff him. We've got backup on the way." Bobby's eyes bounced between the man moaning on the floor and Chris who was still aiming his gun, as if he hadn't heard a thing.

"No," cried Piper, hobbling forward and lunging for the gun her father had placed on the end table. She pointed it with shaking, tired hands as the tears poured out of her eyes. Lindsey drew her weapon again and, with no choice, aimed it at Piper. Bobby did the same, pointing his at Chris.

Bobby fought to process this. He looked down at the doubled over bleeding man, he was motionless but alive. He was unarmed, injured, the threat had been neutralized. What was his move here? The cop in him knew it was his job to take the criminal into custody. Anyone pointing a weapon at another human, regardless of the crimes committed, needed to be talked down, detained, or disarmed. He tried to keep his voice soft, but he barely recognized the woman before him, struggling to reason with her sad, defiant eyes. "Piper, you don't have to do this. Lower the gun, hand it to me. He can't hurt you anymore. He can't hurt anyone."

"You don't get it, Bobby," Piper wailed. "Your dad is somewhere doing someone's taxes right now. Your mom is probably food shopping. This is something you'll never be able understand. As long as he's alive, I won't ever be free. I'll spend the next two years reliving this, testifying against him. If he walks out of here, he'll haunt me forever." She steadied her hands and took a step closer. Lindsey looked over at Bobby, asking with her eyes if he had a plan. He didn't.

Chris softened his voice and chose his words carefully. "Piper, sweetheart, give Bobby the gun. Everything's going to be okay, I promise. Just hand the gun to Bobby."

Piper's face twisted with confusion. Chris was the one who had shared with her his own burdens. He knew better than anyone what she was facing. But he smiled at her sincerely, nodding his head in reassurance. It was enough to distract her, to bewilder her, and she lowered the gun to her side. Lindsey came up behind her slowly, whispering words of comfort, and secured the weapon that was hanging loosely in Piper's shaking hand.

"Take her outside," Chris said, his voice returning quickly to a steely tone. And that's when it hit everyone in the room. He wasn't telling Piper that she should let this man live, he was telling her that she didn't need to kill him herself. That he would do it, that it would be all right, because he'd handle it.

Lindsey put Piper's arm up over her shoulder and helped her out the front door. Under normal circumstances she'd never leave an officer in a room with an armed man whose intentions were to kill someone, but this was a unique situation, and getting Piper out of that room was crucial.

Bobby pointed his weapon back at Chris, as much as his instincts begged him not to. "Chris, you need to lower your weapon. We are going to place him under arrest. He is going to get the death penalty. Let the system do its job."

"Do you know how many years the average person spends on death row? Ten. You want to marry that girl? Have a family with her? You have the opportunity for her to start healing today. Your other choice is for this to be a part of her life for the next ten years. I'm not asking you to pull the trigger, I'm asking you to let me do it."

Bobby had no more words. No argument. He could cite every law they'd be breaking, every ethical guideline he'd be ignoring. But his heart hadn't thought of the things Chris had just said. He hadn't considered the difference between Piper's father dying here today as opposed to being arrested. Before this moment they both seemed equal in finality, but now he saw the truth. There was a big difference between him leaving in cuffs versus a body bag. Bobby felt demons from his past encircling him, taunting him as he wrestled with his conscience. This moment *was* Bobby's history. This was what created the rift inside him. He'd stood here before, much younger, and let someone tell him that killing was the best, no, the only answer. That choice, the one to be complacent in the face of something he believed was wrong, had broken him, and the only way he was able to repair his fragile young soul was to promise himself he'd never do anything like it again. But here he was considering it.

Could he really relive the biggest mistake of his life and not change the outcome by changing his actions? Was he willing to turn away from his highest ideals, all because someone was, once again, telling him it was the right thing? He couldn't give his approval. He couldn't tell Chris to do it. But he couldn't bring himself to take the necessary actions to prevent it either. Chris read his silence as hesitant permission. "That day, when I stood with my gun pointed at the judge and you talked me out of it," he said, walking with purpose toward the trembling man on the floor, "you were right, and I walked away from that for you. I did that for you." He put the barrel of his gun to the man's temple. " I'm doing this for *her*."

"It doesn't matter if he pulls that trigger." Piper's father groaned as he locked eyes with Bobby. He'd lost a good amount of blood and his voice was shaking but still ominous. "I've already wrecked her. You couldn't put her back together even if you wanted to." With that Bobby looked away from both of them. All he could do was lower his weapon and take a step backward, silently granting his permission.

Chris knew there was only one way to silence a madman. He pulled the trigger and Bobby winced as Piper's father crumpled. He lay limp, his eyes wide open. The manic look was gone, and now he was just a dead man.

Lindsey came back quickly through the door. "You good?" she asked, stepping quickly to Bobby's side. His head was full of questions, his face loaded with panic. Lindsey looked over the table to the lifeless corpse. "The son of a bitch killed himself? That's probably for the best," she muttered flatly.

Bobby looked over at her, perplexed. He wondered, did she really think he had killed himself? She was a better, more astute cop than that, wasn't she? Her response cleared the air.

"Bobby, you really think this guy deserves a taxpayer-funded cell and three meals a day? He's wrecked so many lives, and nearly killed two people you love. I know you think there's one right way to do everything, but I can tell you this is the best thing that could have happened. Now let's get our story straight."

She moved toward Chris and took the gun from his hand. She pulled a rag from her pocket and wiped the prints off it. She placed it in the hand of the dead man. "We entered the cabin and engaged the man. He had already been shot while Piper tried, unsuccessfully, to wrestle the gun away from him. He tied her down to ensure she could no longer resist. He cut into her leg before his blood loss caught up with him. When we arrived he was sitting on the floor, in shock. We secured the victim, I removed her from the cabin, you approached to secure the assailant, and he killed himself."

Bobby's eyes were wide with a look of disbelief, almost fearful how quickly she'd concocted the story and how confidently she'd laid it out. "Don't look at me like that," she snipped. "What's done is done, and all we can do is get our side of this squared away so we can put it behind us."

"What about the fingerprints all over this place?" Bobby responded, looking at Chris. "They'll know you were here. And the gun, it's yours. It's registered to you," Bobby said, trying to run through all the forensic land mines they could hit.

Chris snickered a little. "That's not exactly how it works in my world. The gun isn't registered to me. The serial number is filed off. And this place *should* be loaded with my fingerprints. I own it. This is my cabin. I didn't feel right letting you two come back to Edenville on your own, so I got on the earliest flight out. When I arrived, I heard what happened. I knew Piper had been taken, and I had a description of the car. I came here to get some supplies before going to look for Piper, and lo and behold, here they were. If that isn't divine intervention, I don't know what is. God was watching out for that girl today."

"I hate to break up your prayer circle here, but I hear sirens coming. I know who you are," Lindsey said coldly, meeting Chris's eye, "and unless you want to join all your recently incarcerated buddies, you need to take off."

Chris nodded. "I like this girl," he said, smiling at Bobby whose eyes were fixed on the corpse staring back at him. Chris truly felt he'd done the right thing, but whether or not Bobby could get right with it, he wasn't sure.

"Bobby, I—" Chris started that statement without really knowing how to finish it. He wasn't sorry for doing what he'd done, but maybe he was sorry that Bobby couldn't understand it.

Bobby finally shook his gaze from the dead man and mentally rejoined the room. Chris was right. Ending this nightmare now meant the healing could start immediately for Piper. Didn't she deserve that more than her monster of a father deserved to live? Chris had nothing to gain from this and everything to lose. It wasn't a sadistic killing; it was a merciful one. He tried hard to convince himself. But hadn't the scenario of his childhood seemed just as justifiable, equally as *right* in that moment? Yet it wasn't long before everything fell apart, and he assumed this would be no different. "You'd better go

Chris. I'll tell her goodbye for you."

"Go already," Lindsey shouted, shoving Chris toward the door. Turning to Bobby she added, "We need to get Piper up to speed. We're in this together, so I need to know—you're good with it?"

"Yeah," Bobby said with forced certainty. "I'm on board." He wasn't going to say anything, not tonight… not right now… but he didn't know how he'd live with it, how any of them would live with it.

Chapter Nineteen

AS THE TWO EMTs lifted Piper into the back of the ambulance, Bobby felt himself finally relax a little. She was physically stable now that her bleeding had stopped. Emotionally, though, he wasn't sure how any of them would manage. When Lindsey had brought her out of the cabin, and left when she heard gunfire, Piper had crumpled. She slid down the side of the car and felt herself go numb. Maybe it was shock setting in, blood loss, or maybe it was the realization that someone in that cabin was likely dead. She lay there wondering if Bobby had shot Chris or if Chris had shot her father. Regardless, she knew her life and her future had just changed dramatically.

Bobby pulled himself into the back of the ambulance and sat down next to her, pulling her cold hand up to his chest. "How you doing?" he asked, knowing it was a dumb question.

"I feel free," she whispered quietly, the corners of her mouth rising slightly in a smile. She squeezed his hand with the little energy she had and then closed her eyes. The bright overhead lights of the ambulance were too much for her.

"Officer Wright," shouted someone from outside the ambulance just as the doors were about to close. Bobby jumped, still on edge, feeling at any moment their story would be called into question. The medic stopped short of slamming the door and let the man come over. Bobby didn't recognize him, but judging by his black suit and tie it was safe to assume he was FBI.

"I'm Special Agent Miles Stanley. I need to get your statement about the scene at Saint Julian's Church as well as what transpired here. Can you come down and talk with me please?" The man had salt and pepper hair and features that screamed *I'm the boss*. He clearly wasn't often told no. He seemed like a man who got what he wanted, but Bobby was about to throw him a curve ball.

"I'm going to the hospital with my girlfriend. I've given my statement to the Edenville detectives. If you need more than that, hop in."

"Officer Wright, you know this protocol. You need to be debriefed, and we need to get a full written statement of your account. You know the rules."

Bobby felt himself smile a little inside, though outwardly his jaw was set in a hard line of determination. This is what everyone around him was constantly saying, and now, though not on the grand scale, in this instant he finally understood it. "To hell with the rules. I'm going to the hospital with Piper. Now either get in or stand back." Bobby released Piper's hand and made a move for the ambulance door, fully prepared to close it on the man's head if that's what it took.

"I'll see you at the hospital," Agent Stanley managed to yell as the ambulance doors slammed shut. He stepped backward, resigning himself to being trumped by love.

Piper cracked open her eyes and reached for Bobby's hand again. "Did I just hear the straight-laced goodie-two-shoes cop say *to hell with the rules*?" She looked over at the stocky, bald EMT currently taking her blood pressure and smiled. "You better turn down my pain medicine, I'm hallucinating."

In spite of this lighthearted moment, things were not miraculously fixed between them. They weren't suddenly healed and compatible, now seeing the world the same way. The death of her father may have helped Piper as an individual, but she wasn't sure what it would mean for her and Bobby as a couple. She knew being witty didn't mean she was going to come out of this unscathed, but right now she needed a little cheerfulness.

As they unloaded Piper at the hospital, Bobby found a quiet corner and pulled his phone from his pocket. Judging by the seventeen missed calls, he knew Michael, Betty, and Jules had no doubt been wondering what was going on. They'd be desperate for an update.

"Michael, I've got some news," Bobby said, not sure where to start. "I'm sorry we didn't check in, but things got a little crazy here. Piper was taken by her father and Carlson was injured trying to stop him. He took her to Chris's cabin, and we were able to get Piper back safely. Her father is dead." The words clogged in his throat like he was swallowing sawdust. "I don't have an update on Carlson yet, but Piper is all right."

"We're fine here. I'm glad to hear Piper is doing okay. And when you find out about Agent Carlson let us know. I don't know if you ended up seeing him or not, but Chris flew back to North Carolina in case you needed some help. We're obviously going to stay here with little Chris until he gets back." Michael said evenly. Bobby could imagine that Michael had Betty and Jules staring at him like hawks. He was probably trying to keep his composure in the face of the big new for their sake.

Bobby let out an exasperated breath. "We saw Chris. He saved her life. He got to her just in time. It's a long story. I'll fill you in later. Piper is getting checked out, and I'm going to try to get an update on Carlson. I'll talk to you guys soon." Bobby hung up his phone and headed for the front desk.

After a few minutes of showing his badge and explaining the situation, the two officers perched outside Agent Carlson's intensive care room decided to let Bobby in. As he pushed open the door he was shocked to see the normally invincible agent lying helplessly against the white sheets of the hospital bed. The door pulled open behind him and in walked a doctor, a large chart in hand. He was a short, big nosed man with curly white hair, and seemed completely engrossed in the information he was reading.

"Oh, sorry," he said looking up from his chart. "I'm Dr. Siegel, the intensive care physician. I'll let you visit. I can come back."

"No, please stay, it's no problem. Is she going to be okay?"

Bobby pulled up the chair next to Carlson's bed and sat solemnly. He was expecting her to look more like she did the last time he'd seen her—hurt, but conscious. That was not the case. She was taking short, shallow breaths, and her skin was ashy and faded.

"I'm sorry to say she isn't. The gunshot wounds she sustained involved several of her major organs. We performed surgery to try to repair them, but unfortunately the damage was too extensive. We're all actually amazed that she's hung on this long. It's good that you're visiting with her. They told us she had no family. There have been a few other colleagues of hers that have come by, but they didn't stay. It won't be long now, it's good that you'll be with her."

"Isn't there any more you can do?" Bobby asked, surprised by the doctor's seemingly pessimistic attitude.

"There would be, but she has a do-not-resuscitate order. She doesn't want any extraordinary measures taken post-surgery to keep her alive. In her case, these measures might buy her a few more days, but she would be completely reliant on machines. She didn't want to live, or die, like that. Like I said, with her stats the way they are, I'm amazed she made it through the afternoon. She must be hanging on for some reason." The doctor hung the chart by the door, adjusted some buttons on the machine by Carlson's bed, and then slipped quietly out of the room.

Bobby leaned in and started a conversation with Carlson even though he knew she wouldn't reply. "I guess it's easy to figure out what you were holding on for. You said you wanted to live on a planet where he wasn't free to hurt anyone else. Well, you did it. He's dead, and you're alive." To Bobby, Carlson's lying here dying only deepened his belief that trying to fight evil with evil never worked. He'd lived it as a child, and now here it was again. A life, many lives, ruined by the backward philosophies of ignoring a justice system that had been working quite well for decades. "I'll never understand what you did, or how you managed to justify it. I don't like how you played the game, but you won, and that counts for something. I want you to know that I don't intend to tell anyone what you told us today. It isn't because I agree with what you did or that I forgive you. I just can't see who it helps. You did your job well for a long time, and then you screwed it up. You were going to try to make it right. You died trying to protect someone." He paused, thinking of what he'd be doing right now if Piper hadn't survived. It chilled him to the core to even consider it.

"Those things count. You're going to go out a hero, and maybe you haven't completely earned that, but maybe you haven't earned the alternative either." Bobby hung his head and said a prayer, something he hadn't done in far too long. "I've got my own blemished conscience, and I'm not really in a position to judge you." Then he sat silently, listening to the ticking of the clock and the beeping of the machines until an hour passed and the periodic beeping turned to a steady, long beep. He knew what that indicated. As the door to her room swung open and nurses poured in, Bobby reached for Carlson's hand. She'd made mistakes, but she didn't deserve to die alone.

As he left Carlson's room and made his way back toward Piper's, Bobby realized he'd need to break the news to her. If he had mixed feelings about Carlson's death he could only imagine how Piper would feel. Just one more emotional conundrum to tackle together.

Chapter Twenty

PIPER HAD HOPED all of this would be easier. Maybe she and Bobby would instantly fall into each other's arms now that the chaos was over. She would feel healed by the death of her father. Maybe she wouldn't have lasting effects concerning the impact of Carlson's betrayal. Perhaps her new life would start now and it would be perfect. But there was a reason she avoided optimism; it often fell short of reality. There was still so much to be worked out between her and Bobby, much of it made worse by what happened in the cabin. There were moments it was clear Bobby was tormented by what he'd allowed to happen there. The anxiety of it being uncovered was written on his face every time they'd been forced to recount it for one agent or another. She worried that things may never settle down for them. Maybe he blamed her for putting him in that position and maybe she couldn't overlook his hesitation that day. Silence kept creeping up between them, and the longer it lingered the more doubt grew in her mind.

Her father was dead. She didn't understand how that could feel like both a weight lifted from her and a piece torn from her all at the same time. She was suddenly the child of no one. There was a magnificent freeing feeling that would be quickly punctuated by a haunting loneliness. She didn't yearn for her father, frankly she never had. But she was now related to no one. She knew no one who shared her DNA. That was a very isolating concept.

And then there was Carlson, the complicated contradiction that kept challenging Piper's mind. Was she angry at her still? Was there a part of her that understood why Carlson did what she did? Maybe even a different part of her that was happy Carlson had drawn her father in and brought this all to a close? The mixture of feelings swirling around Piper was too much for her to bear. She couldn't sort them out or separate them long enough to decide how she felt.

"You want me to deliver her eulogy?" Piper asked incredulously, looking back and forth between Agent Stanley and Bobby.

"She has no family. None of us knew her that well. You were one of the last people to speak with her that day. She was shot trying to protect you. I think she'd like it if you said a few words at her funeral tomorrow." Agent Stanley barely looked up from his paperwork, not wanting to make it look like he was giving Piper much choice.

She'd gotten the all clear from her doctors and was minutes away from being released from the hospital. Betty, Jules, and Michael were driving back from Illinois in their rental car and due to return to Edenville shortly. They planned to join her and Bobby for celebratory moonshine at Betty's. Then suddenly Agent Stanley decided to spring this on them along with some last minute paperwork.

"So, I'll expect you to have something ready for tomorrow then," he said nonchalantly. "Now, please sign right here."

"What is it?" Bobby asked skeptically. The paperwork they had all filled out was endless, requiring them to recount what had happened again and again. But up until this point there weren't many things they needed to sign.

"There is no imminent danger to her, so she can now resume her old identity. She's free," he said, smiling for the first time since they'd met him. He slid the paper across the rollaway hospital table that had acted like a desk for them all over the last few days.

"Don't sign that paper," Betty said bursting into the room and racing over to Piper for a hug. "This child is Piper Anderson, and she's got no interest in being anyone else."

"Betty!" Piper shot up, opening her arms for a hug. "I thought we were going to meet at your house."

"We saw Bobby's truck parked out front and figured these big city bureaucrats were in here slowing you down. Good thing I came when I did. You're not thinking of giving up your name, are you? Going back to New York?"

Piper wanted to say; *I'm going to live the rest of my life as Piper. I'm not looking back, even for a second.* But a part of her was hesitant. It wasn't because she wanted to move back to New York. She didn't want to go back to being who she was before, but she didn't feel ready to be the person they all wanted her to be. Did signing this paper mean she was committing herself to being whole? She still felt broken, and signing something that said she was free of her past—free to choose where she lived and decide what she wanted—was terrifying. She'd never really had freedom. As restrictive as that was, it was all she knew. Now faced with limitless possibilities and choices, she was completely overwhelmed.

"All this paper is saying is that you could if you wanted to. You are free to maintain the identity that was given to you when you relocated. Many people make that choice." Stanley was back to being his dry, serious self again. The smile had vanished quickly.

"Maybe you should have your lawyer look at it?" Michael laughed. He and Jules were leaning in the doorway of her hospital room.

"If I could find a half decent one, maybe I would." At the sight of all the people she loved, in one place, Piper felt calm returning. She reached for the pen and signed the paper, not because she'd come to terms with any of it, but because no one would understand if she didn't sign it. Her explanation, her fear, wouldn't sound logical to any of them.

"Well, I think it's high time we go get ourselves three sheets to the wind," Betty hooted, and the group agreed in unison.

"We all need a strong drink and a good night's sleep," Bobby said, trying to stretch out the aching in his back from sleeping in a hospital chair.

"I doubt there'll be much sleep for y'all. You know what they say, lips that touch liquor touch other lips quicker. Just no one go making me any grandbabies tonight. I need a good long rest before I can handle any more commotion."

"I think we both have a good long vacation coming to us, Ma. We've been away from our jobs for weeks without giving them so much as a phone call." Jules didn't want to dampen the mood of the moment, but she'd been stressing about it for some time.

"It's already been taken care of," said Agent Stanley. He was so stiff, they'd almost forgotten he was in the room, the same way you might overlook a houseplant or an end table. "You'd be surprised what a call from the FBI can get you. Both your jobs are waiting for you if you want them. No reason you should be punished for events you couldn't control."

The room was silent. Agent Stanley didn't look like a man you'd hug, not without some consequence, and no one knew quite what to make of his generosity or how to respond. They all looked at Betty, knowing she'd be able to manage something.

"That was mighty kind of you, Miles. I knew you couldn't be as bad as you look," Betty said, either not grasping the fact that it wasn't customary to use an agent's first name, or simply rejecting the idea as ridiculous.

In his normal robotic way, Agent Stanley stood, nodded his head, and made his way to the door. "We'll see you tomorrow, Agent Stanley. I'll have something written up for Agent Carlson. Thank you again for all your help," Piper called as he rounded the corner from the room. He was an uptight, all-business agent who clearly needed a good laugh, or a good lay. It was ironic now how Piper could see people and look at them with pity when their lives lacked more depth, considering not too long ago that was how she lived. Maybe it would be the way she'd return to living.

"What in the hell are we still doing here?" Betty asked, gingerly pulling Piper to her feet. "I brought lasagna back in the cooler from Chris's house. Let's go pop that baby in the oven and drink until we can't tell our feet from our hands."

They piled into their cars and headed for Betty's house. Pulling up the long dirt driveway hadn't lost its appeal at all for Piper. It was still like passing through the gates of a secret garden, a hidden sanctuary where she'd first learned to love.

They climbed out of their cars, and after starting a fire, changing their clothes, and filling their glasses, they all settled onto the porch. The lasagna was cooking, and the drinks were flowing. The world was right again.

"Okay this is everyone's last chance," Jules said, looking accusingly at all of them. "Any more deep, dark secrets to tell us about? Any more skeletons in those closets? I'm not sure I can take another adventure with you people."

They all looked over at Piper, half joking, but secretly wondering if anything else could come crashing down on them. "No," she scowled, looking insulted. "This is it, I swear. My problems just died with my father. I've got no one else in the world but you guys, which means no other drama coming."

"You do have us, Piper, you know that, right?" Betty asked as she settled into her rocker. "This commotion is all behind you now, and you can finally just be here. We hope that means you'll be staying here in Edenville, staying a part of our family."

No one expected the hesitation, the long pause as Piper wrestled to find the words. "I thought I knew exactly how I would feel when I was free of all this, but it's not as clear as I imagined." She felt like she was physically striking these people, like she'd crossed the porch and slapped each of them in the face. But if that was how they were feeling, they weren't showing it. They still had empathy in their eyes.

"No one thinks this is going to be easy, Piper. You've got a slew of stuff to figure out, and there ain't one of us here who can begin to imagine what you need. But what we can do is keep reminding you we're here when you need us." Betty wanted to hold Piper now, sit her right down on her lap and rock her like a baby until the hurt stopped. But she knew that wasn't what Piper wanted.

"I am so grateful I found all of you. I want to feel better. I wish I knew exactly what's right for me right now, but I don't. What I do know is that I wouldn't be sitting here—I probably wouldn't be alive—if I hadn't met you all. I know I'm not perfect," she sighed, as she looked over at Bobby, "and I'm not sure why you guys care about me, but I'm glad you do."

Betty pulled her quilt over her legs and did what she did best, comforted. "It's not your job to be perfect, Piper. It's our job to love you like you already are. That's what family is all about. All this stuff that happened to you—we can't make it go away. You're going to have a long journey ahead of you, and all we can do is come along for the ride if you want us. You'll make mistakes, we all will. But if our hearts are in the right place we'll get through it." Piper knew this wasn't just a speech about friendship, it was one directed at Bobby and Piper. It was words of advice for their love from someone who'd had and lost her own soul mate. Someone who never took it for granted and didn't want them to either.

They all chatted comfortably as they spent the next couple hours drinking themselves into a warm, numbing stupor. They'd spend the night here, not because they had to, not because they were hiding from some imminent danger, but because they wanted to. That was the true sign of their connection to each other. When all the reasons forcing them to stay melted away, they still chose to be together.

Chapter Twenty-One

"WE MISSED THANKSGIVING," Betty whined. "How do you miss a holiday? This is like a crime against humanity." She stomped her heavy high-heeled foot on her kitchen floor in protest. She had pulled on a black dress, her funeral dress. In Edenville it was expected that the whole town show up at a funeral, because, in one way or another, everyone knew everyone even if there were multiple degrees of separation. Showing support by attending funerals was part of the town's culture. This made Betty very well prepared for the laying to rest of someone. Even though Agent Carlson hadn't been her favorite person, even though this was just a memorial service since Carlson's body would be sent back to New York to be buried, and in spite of the fact this was not a full Catholic funeral mass, she intended to go and show her respect. She had her hair up, and artfully secured to the side of her head was a dainty pillbox hat with a lace drape. Piper couldn't help but smirk at Betty's temper tantrum. She didn't often fuss over things that didn't go her way, but this had clearly annoyed her.

"We were all a little preoccupied. We were driving back here, Piper was in the hospital. There will be other holidays, Ma. It's just one Thanksgiving." Jules, too, was wearing a classic black dress with a gray sash around her waist. She'd pulled her hair up as well and grabbed a small black clutch to carry with her. They both looked beautiful, and in similar outfits their resemblance to each other was almost spooky.

"This family does not miss holidays," she shouted back. "We have traditions that date back over a hundred years. The way I stuff the turkey with apples and rosemary, do you think I just came up with that one day? That is my great-grandmother's recipe. This is truly a disaster."

Piper remained silent as the "catastrophe" unfolded. She felt responsible for the uprooting of their lives and the resulting missed holiday. She sat at the kitchen table attempting to look as small as she could, but Betty caught her.

"Why aren't you dressed yet? The boys will be back here any minute to pick us up. You can't go in jeans and a sweatshirt." Betty looked down at her watch and then back up at Piper.

"I don't have anything to wear. I've never been to a funeral. I don't even really know what you do at one." Piper's eyes darted away. She knew how silly that sounded considering this was not the first time her life she had crossed paths with death.

"You didn't go to your mother's funeral?" Jules asked in disbelief.

"I don't think she had one. I was in the hospital. I think she was cremated maybe. I don't really know." The thought had never occurred to Piper, but now she could see the sadness in living a life that left no one to mourn you when you were gone.

"Look at me going on about a dumb old holiday. Trivial thing, really. Jules, take Piper upstairs and get her one of your funeral dresses. She's got a big speech to deliver up there today, she needs to look the part." Betty sat down next to Piper and stroked her hair. "You go on and get dressed. Jules and I have been to loads of funerals, we'll show you the ropes." She leaned over and kissed Piper's forehead.

Once a dress had been chosen, her hair had been pulled up into a respectable bun, and she'd selected a pair of tasteful heels, Piper felt ready. Well, physically anyway. She still hadn't quite come to terms with the fact that she was about to stand at a podium in front of a group of mostly strangers and eulogize a woman she genuinely didn't like. She hadn't forgiven all of Carlson's cruel words or selfish mistakes. She hadn't even really come to grips with Bobby's proposal to let sleeping dogs lie and not bring to light what Carlson had told them that day, nor expose her for the crimes she committed. Piper knew it took a lot for Bobby to even consider overlooking such an egregious mishandling of the law. It was a step forward in Bobby's growth and understanding of using his heart rather than his head, and she certainly wasn't going to be the one to snuff that out.

"You look really nice," Jules said, coming up behind her and fastening the necklace Piper was struggling with. "Do you know what you're going to say?"

"I wrote something, but I'm still not really sure. I told you, I've never been to a funeral before. I don't know what people are expecting me to say."

Jules reached over to her pink dresser and opened a small box. In it was a white folded piece of paper. She carefully opened it, and smoothed it on the desk in front of Piper. "This is what I said at my father's funeral. Well, what I tried to say—I cried my way through most of it."

"Will you read it to me?" Piper asked, not wanting to just see the words but hear them from someone who'd meant them wholeheartedly. Stan was like a familiar ghost to Piper; she had never met him, but somehow, through stories and pictures, she felt connected to him. Helping to bring the men who had killed him to justice made that connection even deeper. She wasn't there the day Stan was buried, she didn't know any of these people back then, but she often wished she had. She'd daydream at times about what her life would have been like if she and Jules were sisters, or neighbors maybe. What if living in Edenville was all she'd ever known—what would it feel like to have spent her whole life here?

She closed her eyes and imagined that day, that sad day when Stan was laid to rest. She wanted to hear what it was like to love your father. Her father was being buried now in some unmarked grave with no ceremony. She'd never have the chance to stand up and speak about him. She made a mental correction; she'd never have the burden of speaking about her father.

Jules cleared her throat and gripped the paper tightly, just as she did that day eleven years ago. "Thank you all for coming today. My mother and I are eternally grateful for the support and love you've shown us in this very difficult time. I'd like to share with y'all a story of my father. Something I think sums him up perfectly. When I was seven years old I stole three candy bars from Cherrywood's General Store. Don't worry, Mr. Cherrywood already knows about this, my daddy made sure of that. I walked into my house with a face full of chocolate, and my daddy, with his keen instincts, knew immediately that I'd done something wrong. I think at first he thought I'd just gone and spoiled my dinner by filling my belly with junk, but as he started to question me, I broke. I told him how I'd taken the bars from the shelf and stuffed them in my pockets. Then I'd hidden under the slide at the playground and eaten all three in a row. He looked at me for a long time, letting me stew in my own guilt and fear. He took me by the hand and drove me down to see Mr. Cherrywood. He didn't tell me what I should say, or what I should do. He just stood me in front of the counter I had stolen from and was silent. I cried, sobbed really.

I was so angry with him for embarrassing me, for making me own up to what I had done. I could barely get the words out, but I fumbled my way through an apology and a promise to pay Mr. Cherrywood back for the things I had taken.

I thought my father hated me. I thought his disappointment in me would last forever. But on the drive home, when the silence in the car was too much for me, I asked him if he was mad at me. If he still loved me. He gave me the answer that I'll hold in my heart for the rest of my life. He said, *Baby Bear, it isn't about doing it right all the time, sometimes it's about making it right. What you did in there today, telling the truth and owning up to your mistake, took a lot of courage. Don't you ever ask me again if I still love you—because it's just wasted breath. No matter what you do, no matter where you are, my answer will never change. You've got my love the same way the ocean has the shore. It's always there—the tide can change, the sea can be rough, but somewhere the water always meets the sand. That never changes.* I believe that still today. In the face of all this sadness I still believe my daddy's love is like the water touching the sand. It will always be there for me."

Jules's face was wet with tears, and Piper felt the familiar panic of managing someone else's grief. It frightened her, and Jules knew that. "I'm sorry," she said trying to quickly dry her cheeks. "I know you aren't a fan of all this sappy stuff."

Piper stood, and even though it didn't come naturally to her, she pulled her friend in for a hug.

"I'm sorry I never got to meet him," she whispered, stroking Jules's back the way Betty often did to her.

"He would have loved you," Jules beamed as they broke their embrace. "Well he would have thought you were odd, he would have worried about you corrupting Bobby, and he probably would have tried to convince you to come to church with us, but he would have loved you."

"Jules, I'm afraid." Piper whispered, hanging her head as her own tears came.

"Of giving the eulogy?"

"No, I'm afraid of how I feel. I thought I'd feel differently. I thought I'd be ready to start my life—to be in love. But I don't think I'm ready. I think Bobby assumes that now that everything is behind me I'll be this ordinary person, and that isn't the case. I don't want to disappoint him; I just don't feel right yet. I can tell he doesn't feel the same way he did before all of this either." She hadn't planned this last minute confession, but the worry was suffocating her.

"He'll understand, Piper. He'll wait for you." Jules rubbed Piper's shoulder sympathetically, aching for her friend. The problem was, Piper realized, Jules didn't know what had happened that day in the cabin.

"Girls," Betty called from the bottom of the stairs, "the boys are back, we need to get going." They locked hands and hurried down the stairs together toward the front door. "Oh my word," Jules said, covering her heart. "I know we're going to a funeral and this probably isn't proper, but damn those men look good." Piper leaned on Jules to get a better view of Michael and Bobby as they strode confidently up the driveway. She was right.

Her eyes were fixed on Bobby, his dark hair finally cut back to the short style he normally wore. All the commotion had kept him from getting it cut on his normal every-four-weeks schedule, and he had started to look downright scruffy. His face was clean-shaven, too, and Piper loved how youthful it made him look. He was in a black suit and tie with a crisp white dress shirt underneath. The suit hugged his muscles just right and made his strong shoulders look even broader than usual. He looked gorgeous.

She wanted to fling open the door and run down the steps to him, but something held her back. Something was always holding her back. She wanted Bobby to have a love in his life that was worthy of all he was giving, and she didn't feel like she was that person. Not yet. He deserved more than she could give. She had something now she hadn't had before, hope, and that was a wonderful thing—but it wasn't enough. Not yet.

As they all met on the porch he opened his arms to her and she fell into them, a habit on both sides. Standing there nestled under his strong grip, his cologne surrounding her, she forgot about her talking points, her very well thought out argument about right and wrong. He pulled her in tight and like he always did ran his thumb over the back of her neck. With that, she knew for a moment, he'd forgotten too. For just a second, their love was easy and their opinions didn't stand between them. She loved him, and with a simple hug she knew he still loved her. But the moment she stepped out of his arms and saw his eyes dart away from her, she knew reality was more powerful.

They loaded into Michael's car and drove in near silence over to the grounds where the memorial service would be held. There wouldn't be any room for jokes today, and since that was where the majority of their conversations ended up, they all decided a little quiet time would be better.

The field was filled with people, a sea of black dresses and oversized black hats. Most were Edenville residents who'd never met Agent Carlson before. But in Edenville, a funeral wasn't considered much different than a block party. You went because everyone was going. For a service like today, even those who weren't in the usual funeral circuit had joined. There was a morbid fascination with the recent events surrounding the shooting on the church steps, the arrival of a serial killer, and the final showdown that left him dead. Piper had seen at least three high school students walk by with a shirt that read "Edenville, the sleepy town that just woke up." She wasn't sure if it was meant to be a political statement or a pun, but either way it probably wasn't really fitting for a funeral. And most disgraceful in her opinion were the reporters and camera crews who Betty had rightfully compared to vultures eyeing a freshly squashed possum.

As Piper got her cue and stepped up to the podium, she was surprised by how relaxed she felt. Everything was a little less scary when the person who wanted you dead didn't exist anymore. She took it as a small victory in a much bigger battle she'd been waging with herself.

"First, I want to thank all of you for coming today and helping us honor Agent Lydia Carlson. I know she'd be grateful for the large crowd and all the kind faces. Lydia was a woman dedicated to her job. She worked with a ferocity and gravity that I've never seen before. Some people thought that made her harsh, maybe a little cold. As a matter of fact, there were times I thought that myself. But sometimes it comes down to motivation. Why does one make certain choices? It takes a lot of patience and courage, at times, to look past all the noise and see the *why*.

"Agent Carlson made very difficult choices on a regular basis. The biggest of all was giving her life in an attempt to save mine. I will be forever grateful for what she sacrificed. I don't want her death to be in vain. I want us all to find a lesson in it. And here is what I've come up with. When people you know or love make a choice you just can't seem to understand, something you think you can't forgive, I ask that you try to look past what they've chosen and figure out why they've chosen it. What drives them, what scares them, what are they trying to accomplish? And look for a way to forgive them. A very wise man, whom I've managed to love without ever meeting, once said, 'It's not always about doing it right the first time, sometimes it's about making it right.'

"We're all jaded, we've all wounded someone else, it's unavoidable. It's what we do after that defines our character. Remember this from today, try to make it right."

The crowd seemed to take in Piper's words as they looked to one another with nodding heads and smiling faces. As she stepped down from the podium, Piper rejoined her group. She didn't fall into Bobby's arms, mostly because they weren't spread wide open for her. But, thankfully, Betty's were. For some reason, the fear of being loved by Bobby was ever-present, whereas Betty's maternal love was completely natural to accept. At least she had that. As Betty released her, Piper saw Bobby's sweet smile. It was not the smile of a proud boyfriend or a seductive lover. It was the smile of someone as confused and tormented as she. All she could do was flash back the same awkwardness and hope at some point they'd make sense of it all.

As the ceremony wound down and the crowd started to disperse, Piper saw Agent Stanley walking toward her. Perhaps a goodbye, she thought, trying to ignore the large envelope in his hand.

"Piper," he called, waving at her to join him as he headed to a quieter location.

"Hello Agent Stanley," she said, crossing her arms over her chest and trying hard not to stare at the envelope she was hoping was not meant for her.

"That was a lovely eulogy, Piper. Thank you for doing that. I despise speaking in front of crowds, and if you hadn't agreed to it, I would have had to." He shifted uneasily, straightening his tie awkwardly. Suddenly, it was as if the memory of why he'd just pulled Piper aside had struck him like a lightning bolt. He grabbed the envelope from beneath his arm and stammered, "I almost forgot. I have something for you. On the day Agent Carlson was killed she had this in her possession. It has your name on the front of it. The package was entered into evidence but wasn't deemed pertinent. Normally it takes quite a while to have something like this removed from the case file, but I expedited it. Carlson clearly intended to give it to you that day, and I didn't want red tape to slow it down."

She took the envelope from his hands and held it like a hot coal. She didn't want it. She couldn't handle anything else to think about, to process. "Okay," she quaked, wishing she could throw it back at him and run in the other direction.

He extended his hand to her and she shook it, wincing slightly under his firm grip. "I wish the best for you, Piper. There aren't very many happy endings in my line of work. You're off to a good start here, make the most of it."

"Agent Stanley," she said quietly, looking down at the envelope. "What if I don't know how? What if I'm not built for this? I could handle my life being a mess, it's all I've known. Can I handle normal?"

"I don't know," he admitted, softening his face. "If you need anything, anything at all, feel free to call me. I can't answer that question for you, but there are plenty of other ways I can help when you need it." He nodded his head and turned on his heels as the others approached, exiting before any more niceties were required of him.

"Thank you," she called to him as he strode away.

Betty sidled up to her, and Piper could smell her sweet perfume before she even saw her. "What was that all about?" she asked, staring down at the envelope. A glance around at the group revealed they were all doing the same, and Piper half expected the envelope to catch flame from the heat of their eyes.

"I'm not sure. He said Carlson planned to give this to me the day she was killed. I haven't opened it yet."

"Well get to it," Jules exclaimed, clearly not understanding the weight of what it might contain. Piper had no guesses, but she assumed it wasn't a gift card for a free latte or a massage. It would be something life altering, or in the least, it would be something more to make her question her future. She could feel that. As she tore it open she saw it only contained one sheet of paper with messy scrawled writing. That surprised her, she could have sworn the envelope had been as heavy as lead.

"It's a note." She smirked as she saw the name Isabella written on top, then crossed out and replaced with Piper. It was emblematic of their relationship, Carlson finally coming over to her side regarding her identity.

"Read it out loud," Jules insisted. You could always count on Jules to say exactly what everyone was hoping but didn't feel right saying. Betty slapped at Jules's arm and shot her a look. But then suddenly Piper started to read.

"Dear Piper. I won't say sorry to you, because it sounds too empty. I have every intention of facing my crimes and my mistakes, and I will take whatever punishment is given to me. I deserve it. In lieu of an apology I will give you the only gift I have to give. The truth.

When the leads grew cold on your father's case we revisited every moment of his life to try to find a missing piece. We discovered horrific details of his childhood and how he exhibited countless signs that he would one day grow into a monster. He had an extensive arrest record, something we spent months examining. Then we branched out and did the same research on your mother as well as you. We tried to put every piece of the puzzle together to understand him.

I stumbled upon a discrepancy.

Some math didn't add up. During the time you were conceived your parents were not together. Your father was incarcerated, and your mother was ordered to a sixty-day drug counseling facility. It would have been impossible for them to have had contact with each other. I was fairly certain that he was not your father, so I ran the DNA in the database that was on file from a crime he committed unrelated to the murders against your DNA from the crime scene of your attack. The results were conclusive. You are not his child.

I don't have any more answers than that, though I would imagine from the timeline we constructed that your real father was either an employee or a patient at the facility where your mother was being treated. I don't doubt with your resourcefulness and determination if you put your mind to it you could find out who he is.

I know this will not heal all your wounds, nor do I imagine it will endear you to me either. That isn't my intent. I only wish it helps you leave behind any worries that you, too, are the monster your father was. You don't hold any of the evilness that he does. I can assure you, as a person who has spent the best part of her life chasing it, you are not afflicted with even an ounce of it."

Piper let the paper fall from her hand, and it danced slowly to the ground. How could it be possible to not be able to pinpoint your own emotions? How can excitement and sadness twist themselves together so tightly that you can't break them apart long enough to feel them individually?

Tears streamed down her face, but if someone were to ask if they were tears of sadness or joy, she wouldn't have been able to answer. Could you cry them both at the same time?

The group around her stood like statues, holding their breath, not sure if they should congratulate her or console her. Betty finally let the weighty implications of the letter sink in. She searched her mind for wisdom, something that would help Piper.

"Well ain't that the berries," she said, her face too even for anyone to figure out what the saying meant. Were the berries a good thing or a bad thing?

Piper's face, bemused for a moment, broke into an odd smile. She appreciated Betty's noncommittal attempt at comforting or congratulating. "Yes, Betty, that certainly is the berries." Piper stepped over the letter as if it were a land mine and looked back at all of them. "Let's go have that Thanksgiving we missed. I'm dying for some turkey."

Jules hung back a few steps and leaned down for the paper. She folded it and tucked it into the pocket of her coat. Piper might not want to read these words again today. She may not be ready for them tomorrow. But someday she'd want to see the letter again, and Jules would keep it safe until then.

Chapter Twenty-Two

SO THIS IS what a holiday is supposed to be like, Piper pondered as she watched Betty scurry around the room. Everyone was in his or her usual spot around the table, but this time it was set beautifully. The burnt orange tablecloth and chocolate brown placemats had belonged to Betty's mother. The candlesticks were heirlooms, the source of which no one in her family could agree upon—unlike the salt and pepper shakers, one a pilgrim and one a turkey, bought new when Jules was a toddler. The food was piled high. Homemade mashed potatoes sat enticingly in a large blue ceramic bowl, and Piper was certain they wouldn't be thrown across the room the way they had at her house so many years ago. The turkey was a golden crispy brown, and the aroma of it filled every corner of the house. Cranberry sauce, gravy, stuffing, and yams all occupied matching holiday dishes.

"Bobby, will you say grace?" Betty asked as she joined them at the table and draped her napkin over her lap.

Bobby dropped his head and contemplated giving the standard bless-this-food grace he knew Betty would reject. Instead he cleared his throat and attempted to give one worthy of this non-holiday holiday.

"Thank you, Lord, for this food we are about to enjoy and the company we share. This time last year we never could have imagined who would be sitting with us and what we would have come through in order to be here together. Bless us all in the coming year, and help us make the right choices in our lives. Help us find our way. Forgive us, Amen."

The whole group, besides Piper who didn't know she was supposed to, gave a resounding amen. She couldn't look past

Bobby's punctuation of grace, his request for forgiveness. It was clear now, more and more each moment that passed, he was tormented. She'd put him in a place he never wanted to be and all because of her.

As the food was passed around and the plates filled, everyone smiled with anticipation. "Are you going to go look for your real dad?" Michael asked as he handed the bowl of potatoes to Piper. "I have a few contacts up in New York who might be able to get you started. Let me know and I'll reach out to them."

"I'm not sure I want to find him. I mean, he can't possibly be worse than the man I thought was my father for all these years, but I can't think of a scenario where he'd be an upstanding guy. He was either an employee of a drug facility who had an affair with a patient, or he was a patient with a drug problem. I don't like those odds. I feel relieved knowing I'm not biologically related to a serial killer. Maybe I should just count my blessings and pretend I don't have a father."

"That's taking quite a gamble," Betty said, filling her glass with wine. "You're talking about who someone was twenty-five years ago. None of you are quite old enough to realize how much can change in that time, but I am. You may find something wonderful if you go looking for it. My mama used to say, 'You block your dreams when you allow your fear to grow bigger than your faith.'"

Piper smirked a little, "Well my mother used to say, 'Every man I've ever met is a lying, cheating piece of garbage who only wants one thing.' I don't think that bodes well for my real father being Prince Charming. I haven't ruled out the idea of looking for him, I just feel like I have things here I need to figure out first."

"Well, when you're ready," Jules said, meeting Piper's eye, "we'll all help you. You wouldn't have to go through it alone. But if I get to weigh in a little, I'd say having a father, a real one who loves you, is the most incredible thing in the world. I had to say goodbye to mine way too soon, and maybe you'll find yours later than you expected, but any amount of time with a great father is worth the risk in my opinion. I'd go to the ends of the earth, take whatever risks necessary, to spend one more day with my daddy."

Bobby was noticeably silent through this conversation. He knew the "things she needed to figure out" were about him, and he knew it wouldn't be long before they came to a head.

As the meal finished up, Betty chimed, "Michael and Jules, help me clear the table. Bobby and Piper, why don't you head out to the porch and talk?" And like a well-orchestrated play, all three picked up a dish and disappeared into the kitchen before Bobby or Piper could say a word.

As they found themselves out on the porch again all Piper could think was damn this porch swing. It was just one more splintering tug at her heart, but it felt so good. It was time to talk. Not simple chitchat. They needed to voice the conversation that had remained unspoken since that day in the cabin. They needed to talk about the space growing between them. As Bobby stepped out of the house she scooted over to make room for him. She wasn't angry with him; she didn't want this to be complicated.

"I'm pretty sure no one is coming out until it looks like we've settled things," Bobby groaned as he flopped down heavily beside her. Everyone was well aware of the tension that had grown between Bobby and Piper. They hoped it would be easily fixed. It seemed like common sense—with all the hurdles jumped, love should blossom. But only Michael had been let in on the details of what had happened that day in the cabin. From a legal standpoint it was important to Bobby for Michael to be fully informed and help them navigate any repercussions from the truth being discovered. Michael had actively listened, but didn't interject his opinion about how things transpired. He'd asked questions from his legal perspective: how confident was Bobby that the other officer could be trusted? He wanted to know if there were any cameras on scene, considering Chris's advanced security system. That conversation, the way Bobby approached it, had convinced Piper if he could do it all over again, he'd have handled things differently that day. The regret was eating at him, the worry weighing him down.

She had planned this conversation out, had run it through her head dozens of times. "I'm sorry," she started, staring out into the cold night. "I've been thinking about what your life would be like today if we'd never met. I've brought more turmoil to this town, to all of you, than any one person is worth."

Bobby wanted to reach his hand out and touch her soft cheek. Her skin was always as smooth as a rose petal, and smelled as sweet. He stopped himself, knowing it wouldn't help. Instead he offered, "I wish I could come up with some big speech like Betty does, something to make you realize what you're worth and recognize this isn't your fault, but I just don't have the words."

"Maybe we should just say exactly what we're thinking. This isn't about what I've been through; you'd already accepted that about me. This is about the choice I asked you to make. We always come back to this. You'll never be able to understand why I needed to make sure he was dead. I thought when we left there that day you had found a way to get passed it but really I don't think it had sunk in yet. Every day you move a little further away from me. I feel like I've been watching a crack in the ice get a little wider. You'll always look at me like a monster, and you'll blame me for forcing you to stand by and let something you didn't agree with happen. That's why you can't touch me, can't look at me the way you did before. You can't forgive me."

Bobby fought to keep the lump in his throat from choking him. He was hoping there was a way he could live the rest of his life never having this conversation. He was hoping to wake up one morning and not feel like he'd become something he hated: a liar. But clearly that wasn't going to happen. "I do understand why you felt like you needed him dead. It isn't as though I can't see the advantages. It's the difference between you being here right now or up in New York, preparing to testify. I'm not blaming you for wanting him dead. You're a victim, those are all perfectly natural emotions, but I'm supposed to be able to compartmentalize that anger and fear and execute my job. That's what separates our justice system from others in the world. I'm not mad at you for putting me in this position, I'm mad at myself for not doing my job." He hung his head, staring at his shoes.

"How can you claim to love me and, in the same breath, admit you wish he was still alive? I can't believe that this is just about your job. Because if it is, then all I can think is maybe your feelings for me aren't that strong. I know you idolized Stan and that he did everything by the book, but I can't imagine there would be anything he wouldn't do for Betty."

"You don't know everything about me, Piper. Don't try to put me in this little box and say *this is who you are and this is why*. You aren't the only one with a history. This has nothing to do with Stan. I've seen what happens to people who think they're doing the right thing by ignoring the law. You can't fight fire with fire, because all you do is burn shit down." His voice was layered with frustration. He didn't like being told why he acted the way he did. He was the only one who knew what made him tick.

Piper frowned. "I shouldn't have to guess what you're talking about. Tell me why you can't look past this. Tell me why you think we're doomed now. Do you really think we can't have a happy ending… that it's impossible now?"

"Yes. That's what I'm saying. We're not going to both have this great epiphany one day and meet in the middle."

"We definitely won't if you never explain to me why you feel this way in the first place. Chris killed him because he knew that was what was best for me. He knew it meant the beginning of freedom, because he's been there himself. You've never been there, you won't understand."

"I understand more than you know."

175

"Show me," Piper whispered, leaning down to catch Bobby's downcast eyes. "I showed you mine," she quipped, hoping their old familiar fall back of humor would soften him.

"Piper, I want my biggest problems in life to be us arguing about where to go on vacation or about me going nuts trying to pick the perfect engagement ring for you. I want to be a cop, and want to be in love, and I want it all to work. I want to be myself, the person who went through all my own shit and turned out like this, and I want that to be enough. I can't change everything I believe in to be with you."

"I can accept that," she said, her voice tinny. "But what I can't accept is walking away from this thinking you didn't love me enough. I deserve to know what you're implying. I deserve to hear your story, because at the end of the day it might be the only thing that helps me understand why we can't be together. I deserve to know."

"No one knows, Piper, not even Betty or Jules. I'm a hypocrite for pressuring you to tell me all about your history and then not giving you the same in return. You're right—you do deserve it. Can we go for a walk? I don't want to talk about it here." Bobby's face twisted in a way Piper had never seen before. He looked unfamiliar to her. It was a mix of sadness, fear, and regret.

"Sure," she said, letting him stand and pull her up the way he always did. They stepped down from the porch and started along the side of the house heading toward the backyard. The moon lit the peeling white paint on the house and made it sparkle. The property was sprawling, and Bobby walked her into the unkempt grass of the field beyond the yard. He intended to get so far from the light of the house that it would be too dark for her to see his face as he spoke. He didn't want to have to share this story, but he knew she was right. They'd likely walk away from each other tonight, and the least he could give her was the real reason why. When he felt a safe distance, shrouded by the darkness, he stopped and turned toward her.

"Your father—Roberto," he corrected, "should be in jail right now. He should have been cuffed, arrested, and tried for the crimes he committed, even if that made life harder for you. That is what I believe. I think the fact that I stood by and let Chris kill him is going to ruin me—not just my career but my entire sense of self. I've just let my moral foundation be kicked out from under me. I think we all make promises to ourselves at some time in our lives. I made one to myself when I was nine, and I swore I would never break it. And up until I met you, I did a damn good job of keeping that promise. The second the bullet left Chris's gun, I betrayed myself." Piper had no intention of interrupting him, but she wanted him to know she was there, tuned in—listening. She squeezed his arm and his muscle tightened, but she couldn't tell if that meant he didn't want to be touched or was grateful for the comfort.

"You know I moved to Edenville when I was ten years old. Before that I lived in New Jersey. My mother and father were told they could never have children. They were devastated. They'd dreamed of being parents for years and when they finally accepted the news, they found their own way of making their dream a reality. They became foster parents. They supported dozens of children as they transitioned into adoption or adulthood. And then one day, through some kind of divine intervention, I came along, my mother miraculously pregnant. They'd fallen in love with their role as foster parents, though, and decided they would continue. They began taking on fewer kids, but they still wanted to help where they could.

"When I was seven years old, along came Jedda, the only person I'd ever met who wore a piece of rope as a belt to hold up his pants. He told me it was because he liked to have something he could use when he was climbing trees, but obviously as I got older I realized it was because he was poor. He was thirteen when he first came to live with us. It was supposed to be a very brief placement as the caseworker was trying to find a family for him that was farther away from his old neighborhood, keeping him from going back and getting into trouble. A week turned to a month, then to six months. Jedda was beginning to transition from a smoking, stealing, fire-setting troublemaker into an actual member of our family. It's a rare thing for a teenager who had been through as much as he had to turn a corner like that. But my parents were great. They knew when to push and when to give space. They understood how to love someone who didn't even know he wanted to be loved. When they finally found an alternative foster home for Jedda, my parents asked if he could stay. They asked him if he'd like to stay forever.

"Adopting Jedda was a serious decision but an easy one for my parents and even easier for Jedda. He'd found a place he'd belonged and people who loved him so much that, when given the chance to get rid of him, they'd chosen not to."

"I know how he must have felt," Piper said, speaking into the night, letting her words carry away on the wind.

"I really wanted Jedda to be my brother. I did a project about him in my first grade class, and brought him in for show and tell. All of my parents' friends got together and threw a party for us, celebrating the addition to our family. It was the happiest time of my life. The process of adoption can be long. I think it was nearly a year before the paperwork was final. My parents ran into a snag at some point with his biological parents not wanting to give up their parental rights. They'd both spent time in prison and were deemed unfit, but the courts had been trying to give them an opportunity to make some changes. Those changes never happened. Eventually he was free.

"The day we all walked into court together to become a family, the weather was beautiful and warm that I thought God had turned up the brightness of the sun just for us. We were a family. I had a brother." The word stuck on his tongue, thick in his mouth like peanut butter. Having a brother had made him feel whole, and the joy it brought to his parents was apparent.

"Eleven months," Bobby said, turning himself away from Piper and looking up at the stars. There were hardly any stars to be seen from his home in New Jersey. He stared up at them now to remind himself he was here, not there. He had to assure himself that as painful as this was to recount, as real as it felt, it was only a memory. "Jedda was my brother for eleven months, then something changed. He started to slip back into his old ways. It was subtle at first, but as he approached his fifteenth birthday he was almost unrecognizable. He was caught breaking into the high school, he started a fire behind our house that caused a lot of damage, and he began stealing money. My parents tried to be patient and understanding, but they were at a loss. Something had changed in Jedda, and no matter how many times they asked, he wouldn't tell them what.

"I wanted to know what he was doing, so I followed him one day. I was nine now, and every day after school when he was supposed to be home watching me he would disappear. In my childish mind I had dreamed up all the places he could be going. Maybe he was a superhero and he needed to slip away to save someone. What if he was a spy and he had to check in with his boss?

My mind never traveled to a place as dark as the reality of where he was headed. He walked for forty-five minutes in a direction I had never been before—toward the place where he was born, a place we never really talked about. I can't imagine I was stealthy enough to avoid being seen. I think he knew I was there, and maybe on some level he wanted me to see it. I watched him enter a four-story apartment building with bars on the windows and broken toys strewn carelessly over the lawn. I remember thinking that they must have the coolest mom to let them leave their toys out like this." Bobby smirked as he recounted his naïve impression of the world at age nine.

"It's amazing how our minds work when we're little," Piper said, rubbing a hand down his back. Couldn't this be the same as when Piper opened up to him? Couldn't this bring them closer?

"I went in behind him and followed the sound of his squeaky shoes up the dirty stairs. When he pulled a card from his pocket and started to jimmy the lock, I couldn't stay quiet. I told him to stop, he couldn't steal anymore or he'd get in big trouble. He told me to shut up and come inside as he pushed his shoulder into the door. We walked quietly through the unfamiliar apartment, stepping over piles of clothes and bottles. It was filthy and the whole place smelled like stale smoke."

This description took Piper right back to her own hell. There wasn't a day of her life that her hair hadn't smelled of cigarettes and her clothes weren't pulled out of a wrinkled pile. Her mind raced with what they were heading toward. Was Jedda planning to rob the place? Was he buying drugs?

"He took me to a back bedroom where there was a little girl about my age sleeping on a dirty flattened mattress. She startled awake when she heard our footsteps. She had sores on her arms and legs, and her bones seemed like they were just under her skin. She was so skinny and so dirty that for a second I thought maybe she wasn't a little girl, but an animal. He pulled a sandwich from his pocket, the sandwich my mother had packed him for lunch. The girl moved toward us as if she had forgotten about the chains on her legs that trailed back to the large radiator. I never moved. I watched her eat her sandwich like it was the first thing she'd eaten in months. She didn't speak, not to him, not to me. She ate, and then drank from the soda bottle he'd brought in his other pocket—and then we left.

"The whole thing made no sense to me but it was made more confusing that no words passed between any of us. It was like being part of a well-practiced play only I hadn't read the script. We'd walked halfway back to our house before he spoke. He told me that little girl was his sister and that was where he lived before he came to us. His sister had been put in foster care, just as he had been, but at some point his parents had gotten her back. I don't know if he meant legally, if they had snatched her back, or if she'd just fallen through the cracks. He had found her months ago when he went back to his old house to see if anything had changed. She was being treated very badly, he said, and the only food she seemed to be getting was what he was bringing her.

"I listened to the whole story before I thought of what to say. Then it hit me. It was all okay. We'd tell my mom and dad when we got back to the house, and they'd go get his sister. They'd rescue her and she could live with us, too. I thought that everything would be better by morning and Jedda would be back to his normal self again—back to being my big brother.

"He turned around quickly and shocked me with his anger. He told me we couldn't tell anyone. That it didn't work like that. He made me promise not to say anything to anyone. He warned me that in the real world, the world he was from, his sister would be as good as dead before the system could get it right and get her out of there. Not to mention my parents wouldn't be safe for sticking their nose into something like this. He asked me if I wanted my parents to get hurt or killed. Did I want my house burned down? I didn't, I didn't want any of that. Jedda was so smart.

"I had no reason to doubt he knew what was best. He told me he had a plan and all we needed to do was keep quiet and he'd get his sister safe soon. I asked him three more times on the way home if he thought the police would help us. I told him one time in school an officer had come to visit and told us if we ever needed help we should find a person in uniform and they would take care of it. He didn't react as harshly to these requests, but he just kept telling me it didn't work like that in his neighborhood."

Piper wanted to interject that she could attest to that fact first hand. She had seen plenty of kids ignored by the people sworn to protect them. Even if help was found, sometimes it just didn't happen fast enough. There were plenty of families like Bobby's who created safe havens and new starts for people like Jedda and Piper, but not enough to save all the kids who were abused or neglected, beaten or starved. She wanted to speak up, but Bobby had let her bare her wounds with little interruption, she owed him the same.

"We went home that day and I never said a word to my parents. They'd asked about my day and I told them it was fine.

181

I dreamed about that little girl for the next two weeks. I watched Jedda leave every day with a drink and a sandwich, worrying he'd never come back. Everybody up until this point had always told me the same thing. If you are in trouble, tell a grown-up you trust. I let Jedda convince me that wasn't the case. He came home one day from his long walk to see his sister and he was furious. Something had changed; they had hurt her worse than usual. He told me they'd had a party and hadn't protected his sister from the men there. I didn't understand what that meant at the time but as I got older I realized his sister had probably been raped. He raided our house for any bit of money he could find, even broke my piggy bank and rummaged through my mother's jewelry. I thought maybe he was going to take the money to them and try to buy his sister. Maybe that was how it worked. He disappeared and never returned that night.

"My parents were frantic, asking me if I knew where he was, if he had said anything to me when he took the money. Did I think it was drugs, was Jedda in trouble? I had the answer, but Jedda's warning kept running through my mind. If my parents were involved our house might be burned down, they might come and hurt us. I convinced myself that Jedda would take the money and get his sister. He would bring her home with him and my parents would make it all better.

"The next morning I lay awake in the bottom bunk, waiting for my brother to come fill the top bunk, I realized something must be wrong. He hadn't come back. My parents hadn't heard from him. I dragged my worried self down to breakfast where my mother sat crying and my father was white with fear. A man I had never seen before sat at our kitchen table with a pad in his hand. My mother asked me to sit down, this man had some questions for us.

"I can't remember exactly how he told us, I get mixed up with what I found out that day and what I later heard on the news or from the taunts of classmates. But Jedda had taken the money he had stolen and bought a gun from someone in his neighborhood. He waited until the dead of night and broke into his old house. He shot his parents to death, reloading the gun twice. He freed his sister and called the police. His only request was his sister be placed with his adoptive parents so she could have a good life."

Piper made a mental note that Bobby had never mentioned a sister, and it likely hadn't worked out the way Jedda had hoped.

"Because the investigation was still active, my parents couldn't be granted guardianship of his sister. Everything from that moment on was a downward spiral for everyone involved. My parents were torn to pieces by the investigators and our community. Everyone wondered why they didn't know where Jedda was going, how they'd let him get his hands on so much money. How could they be so blind? Jedda was arrested and arraigned, no bail granted. It was determined he'd be tried as an adult. He pleaded guilty in order to avoid a trial. He knew it wouldn't just be him on trial—it would be all of us, including his sister. He was sentenced to life in prison with no possibility of parole. We never had the chance to see him again. I never got to hug him goodbye, he was just gone one day.

"My parents fought to gain custody of Jedda's sister, but they'd been persecuted so publicly the courts would not allow it. There were times they thought they might even lose me. Six months went by, and as much as we tried to lay low, things kept getting worse. I hadn't told my parents all the things I knew about Jedda and why he went there that day. Because there was no trial, the heinous things they'd done to that little girl would never be brought to light. Jedda refused to see my parents. I like to believe he did that for their sake, but it broke their hearts. There was no closure, not for any of us.

"I started to fall apart under the weight of keeping secrets. I was wetting the bed, fighting at school with anyone who spoke against my family, and I had started to set fires, immediately causing my parents to panic. They didn't want what happened to Jedda to happen to me. They intended to nip it in the bud. They took me to a therapist who spent hours trying to teach me healthy ways to cope with my confusion and sadness, but ultimately it wasn't either of those two things that were driving me. It was my guilt. My lack of action to prevent this, to tell my parents, was crushing me.

"One day a letter came in the mail from Jedda. My father opened it, and my mother and I sat down next to him as he read it out loud. It was an explanation, an apology, but for me it was a dagger to the chest. He made mention of me, asking them not to be upset that I had kept this from them. He took full blame for that, and hoped they understood.

"He unwittingly spilled my secret and, in turn, splintered my family almost into disrepair. My mother cried for hours. My father was too hurt to even be in the same room with me. I had known where Jedda was going, I had known about his sister and I had been told countless times to seek help when I needed it. I knew better. I was selfish; I could have stopped all of this.

"The only thing I could do was promise myself that I would never make that mistake again. I wouldn't allow anyone, even someone I loved, to tell me that doing the wrong thing for the right reason was ever justifiable. I tested that when I met you, you tested me. But I never had any intention of allowing Judge Lions to be killed. I would have done anything to make sure that didn't happen." Bobby felt himself trailing off. He realized he was angry with Piper, which wasn't what he wanted. He tried to refocus on his story, letting her know through his retelling of history why he couldn't come to terms with what he'd done.

"When the school year finished and we had all but destroyed each other emotionally, my father made an announcement. He'd be taking a job down South, and we'd be moving to a new place. A fresh start. Edenville was going to be our salvation. To a certain degree, it was. But all my father did was work, and my mother was painfully depressed. Betty and Stan practically adopted me. You're not the only one who was lost and then saved. The difference is, you're free now. I'm not."

"You were a child, Bobby. You didn't know the repercussions. You were doing what you thought was right."

Piper reached for his face as he turned back toward her, but he pulled her hand down and let it go.

"Two people died that day. My parents have never been the same. Who knows what happened to Jedda's sister. And he'll be in jail for the rest of his life. You're right. I was a child. I didn't realize I had the power to intervene and speak up. But in the cabin, I was a man—a police officer. Do you know what my job tells me I'm supposed to do in that situation? Shoot Chris. He was the threat at that moment. Do you know what I did? I lowered my weapon and might as well have given him permission to end someone's life. I don't know how to go to work tomorrow. I don't know how to look at myself in the mirror. And I don't know how to love you, because you think what happened was the only solution. I don't like what loving you makes me. It wouldn't have been easy for you to let him live, but it would have been right."

Piper was furious, though she didn't know exactly why. Was she mad at Bobby's parents for abandoning him to the point that he would shape his whole life around trying to make it right? Was she mad at herself for the selfishness she'd shown that day, the way she'd left him with no options? "So what, Bobby, do you think you have to spend the rest of your life never stepping a toe out of line to make up for a mistake you made as a child?"

"It's not just atonement for a mistake, it was meant to make sure I never made it again. Now we're all at risk. Chris could be found out and lose his son, lose his new life. Lindsey and I could be prosecuted for conspiracy after the fact, falsifying a police report—trust me the list goes on. And there's a damn good chance you and I will never be the same. Knowing all that, was it still the right thing?"

"Yes," Piper said without hesitation, solidifying the distance between their hearts. "I thought this would free us to be together without history getting in our way, but I didn't know about your history. You never told me."

"Would it have stopped you? If you knew you'd lose me to kill him, would you have stopped Chris?" Bobby didn't need to hear her answer, his heart already knew.

"Why can't we just start over right now? There isn't anything else, it isn't like we're going to ever be in this position again. Do you still love me?"

"I love you in a way that petrifies me. I love you so much that I cut out the best parts of me to make room for you, and now I don't recognize myself."

Piper stood and stepped back from him, fighting tears. His words hit her harder than any punch she'd ever sustained. His sadness was as raw as hers. Neither wanted to say out loud what they both knew was inevitable, but it couldn't be avoided now. "I think we're both saying the same thing here. Love is supposed to be easier than this. I think maybe I need to just move on from here."

Bobby wasn't trying to send Piper away. "You need these people, you need Edenville, Piper. Don't leave just because—"

She waved her hand, not wanting him to say something as trivial as *we're breaking up*, because it was more than that to her. "What, Bobby, don't leave just because we're ripping each other's hearts out? Don't overreact to the worst pain I've ever felt? I love you. And it's killing me that it's not enough. I'm not saying we have other options, I'm just saying don't you dare minimize this. Don't ask me to sit across from you at dinner next week and expect me not to cry my eyes out. I can't be next to you and not love you, you can't ask me to do that." She felt the tears streaming down her cheeks, almost freezing in the air. "I have to go back to New York. Maybe we should just take that time to try—I don't know. Maybe we should get away from each other and see what it's like to be… apart." The word came out as a cough, a cry. She never wanted to say *apart* ever again when it came to them. This was his chance—the moment he'd need to fight for her if he was ever going to.

"Maybe you're right," he whispered, the words too large to say in his normal voice. And with that, Piper felt a piece of her rip. She stormed away—past the house, past the porch where they'd fallen in love, and to her car.

"Piper!" Bobby called, wanting to hold her one last time. He didn't understand how he could love her so deeply and yet need her gone.

As Piper put her car in reverse she saw Jules step out onto the porch, a look of shock spreading on her face illuminated by the yellow porch light. Betty and Michael stepped out behind her and, like sad statues, watched in silence as she drove away. Betty didn't wave this time, she wasn't standing in her normal spot, saying farewell. Instead, one hand was over her mouth, the other over her heart.

Chapter Twenty-Three

"WHAT DID YOU do, Bobby?" Jules fired the accusation at him like a dart. "Why is she leaving?"

"It's complicated, Jules, she just couldn't stay here right now." Bobby's head was low and, though she hadn't seen it in years, she could tell by the arch of his back and the crack in his voice that he was crying.

"Go get her," she demanded, pointing out into the driveway.

"Maybe he won't have to," Michael said hopefully as two headlights cut through the darkness that had gathered as a storm rolled in.

Bobby's head shot up and he squinted to identify the car, maybe she was coming back—maybe. But when the silver pickup truck rumbled closer, he knew it wasn't her.

"Hey," Michael said, stepping off the porch and greeting the man who was a stranger to everyone but him.

"Your receptionist gave me the address, I hope that's okay. I haven't been able to reach you, and she said you might be out here." The two men shook hands and Jules took note of the man's posture, moving like he had a steel rod in his back. Maybe he was an old Marine buddy of Michael's, she thought.

As she saw what stepped out of the car behind the stranger it all became clear, and she smiled. She grabbed the black clutch she'd had at the funeral and fumbled around for the tattered papers from Agent Carlson that Piper had discarded. She listened intently as the man explained the frustrating situation to Michael, and then she made her move. She was with Piper on this all the way, and now maybe they'd have some company.

As Piper drove down the winding road away from Betty's and back toward her apartment, her mind flashed through the events that had brought them to this point. She thought back to the first evening she and Bobby had spent swinging together on Betty's porch, the moment he kissed her on her front steps, the first time they'd made love. And, like always, thoughts of the man she had always believed was her father crept in. He was as invasive as a weed. Every time she'd tried to stomp him out and push him down, he'd pop right back up. She heard his words echoing in her head. *You're just like me, you know this life is a joke; you know you'll never be one of those normal people with a happy life, so why bother? Why fight it?*

Maybe his blood wasn't running through her veins, but he was still the man who had tormented her, beaten her—shaped her. When the voices in her head grew too loud and the tears were coming too fast for her to see straight she pulled her car to the side of the road. She wanted to turn around; she wanted to go back. She wanted to be able to love Bobby and she wanted Bobby to be able to love her. She dropped her head to her steering wheel, her shoulders trembling with the sobs she couldn't control. The cold icy rain had held off all afternoon and started now; all she could think was, bring on the storm.

The rain had begun tapping loudly on her windshield. She'd sit here, she decided, crying while it poured, and when it passed, she'd find a way to pull herself together. She'd let this storm carry her sadness away with it, but for now, as it raged on, she'd give in to it. With her head still propped on her steering wheel and the rain still beating on the roof, she didn't hear the car pull up behind her.

She heard nothing but her own crying and the sad song playing on the radio until the knock on her window that was too loud to be rain, sent her jumping in fear. Jules stood there, soaked through with rain, her black funeral dress clinging to her, and mascara running down her face.

She was still recovering from the shock of being startled, still wiping the hot tears from her face, when Jules shouted over the pounding rain. "Don't go," she yelled, putting her hand to the glass, pleading with her eyes. "Please don't leave."

"I have to. It's over," Piper shouted back through the closed window, her voice cracking with tears. Finally she hit the button and lowered the window.

"No it's not," Jules said, crouching down to get closer to Piper. "He just needs time to figure out how to not be an idiot." Jules didn't realize the magnitude of the situation. She didn't know what happened to Bobby as a child, and she didn't know what happened in the cabin that day. Piper wanted to tell her she didn't understand, but hell, Piper hardly understood any of it either.

Jules put up her finger indicating that she needed a minute. She ran back to her car and returned with a familiar four-legged friend. Bruno came traipsing through the rain to Piper's car. "After you left, Michael's dog-training buddy came by. He said that you ruined Bruno. Whatever you did to him, he won't perform any of his tasks anymore. He's useless to them. I didn't know it was possible, but you *wrecked a dog*," Jules laughed, looking even wilder as the rain whipped her red hair around her face. "He said he tried to find him a few homes, but the people kept bringing him back saying the dog was depressed. The only time he showed any sign of happiness was when he was laying on the blanket you gave him. Apparently he misses you so much he's miserable. Once I heard that, saw this glum dog, I realized I couldn't let you go off on your own."

Piper couldn't fight the happiness that spread across her face as she extended her arm out the window and reached down to scratch Bruno behind the ear. She looked up at Jules, not sure about her next move. Was Jules suggesting she take care of Bruno? Did she even want to take Bruno along? "I need to go. I can't stay here right now. I need to go to New York and get right with some of this. See where it leads me." She reached even further out of the car and got a better hold on Bruno, who seemed elated to be reunited.

"Good," Jules said, shocking Piper with her curt response. Had she really been swayed so easily into letting Piper go? "I've always wanted to see New York. And I think Bruno would be a great city dog." Jules cut in front of the car, the headlights making her wet, red hair glow like fire. She pulled open the door and let Bruno into the back seat, then flopped into the passenger seat, ignoring the shocked look on Piper's face. "Let's go find you a family," she shouted with all her southern charm, slapping Piper on the leg.

"You're coming with me? Right now? Isn't there a whole bag full of beauty products and ten suitcases full of clothes you'd need? You also have a job. "

"Come on, Thelma, we'll get everything we need on the road. Life's too short to stop and pack. And we'll just call in a favor to that nice FBI agent. I'm sure he'll have no problem making sure my job is there when I get home and if not, who cares?" The smile faded a little from Jules's perfect peach lips. "You're like a sister to me, Piper. I'm not ready to let you go. So if you're leaving, I'm coming, too." Jules pulled the note from Carlson out and placed it in Piper's hand.

Nothing about this was logical. They had absolutely no idea where they'd be heading, where they would stay, or what exactly they were looking for. Piper imagined Michael would be furious at their spontaneity and Betty might be slighted for being left out of the fun. There was so much to think about, so much left undone. And when there are that many things telling you not to do something, you only have one choice. Drive.

"Just to be clear, I am definitely Louise. Thelma was the troublemaker," Piper said as she put the car in gear and spun the tires in the icy mud.

Epilogue

AS CHRIS MADE his way through the entrance of the university Admissions Office he knew he was in for it. The good deed he had just finished wasn't going to earn him any points with the banshee of a boss he was about to face. Calling in for two sick days with next to no notice a few weeks into your new job didn't really bode well for a long career. Not to mention Sydney already couldn't stand him. She'd been forced to hire him by the dean of the university. It was part of his relocation that he'd be provided with a cover and employment. They had assumed he couldn't get himself into much trouble at a Catholic university. The idea of that, in contrast to what he had just done back in Edenville, made him laugh.

"Feeling better, Mr. King?" Sydney asked sarcastically. She was a nerd. That was blatantly clear to Chris as he looked at her: studious-looking rectangular, brown-framed glasses, hair half up in a clumsily placed clip, and constantly pursed lips. She was a tight ass, which Chris always smirked about when it came to mind because even in her loose, frumpy slacks he could tell that she actually did have a tight ass. Sydney was everything he had despised in a woman when he was younger. She was strong-willed, opinionated, and in power. His father, well, every man in his life actually, had taught him that these qualities were unattractive and dangerous. Even still, as he took a seat across from her, ready for a lecture on attendance, he found himself half excited.

"I'd like to apologize for calling in sick so soon after starting my position. I know we got off on the wrong foot, and my absence hasn't helped that. So, I'm sorry. It won't happen again." Chris hung his head submissively. This was a new role for him. Since his father died, he'd been the boss. He'd held many lives in his hands, and now he was taking marching orders from some twenty-something geek, and part of him loved it. It was a true testament to how different his life was now. It was proof that things had changed.

"I've worked here for six years," Sydney scoffed, "and I've missed only two days of work after recovering from surgery."

"Nose job?" Chris quipped, feeling like this moment needed some humor. He had just returned from killing a killer. He had just evened up the life for a life debt he had with Bobby. He felt good, and he wanted to laugh. More than that, he wanted to make this prude laugh, too.

"*Excuse* me?" Sydney slammed her hand down on her desk. "I have no idea why they twisted my arm to hire you. You are crude and barely qualified to be part of this department. If it were in my control, I'd have you packing up your desk this afternoon." Sydney's face was crimson, her eyes were boring holes through him, and all he could think was, *Bring it on. Let's see those fireworks in your eyes. Give me all you've got.*

Before she could continue, the door to Sydney's office swung open so hard the knob slammed into the wall behind it. Chris spun around in his chair as a tall blond-haired man stormed in. He had the body of a jock and the vacant dull-eyed look to match. Judging by the look on Sydney's face, a mixture of anger and fear, he could tell the man was looking for her, and things were about to get ugly.

"I can see you're still being a ball-busting bitch, Sydney. Some things never change." The man walked with purpose past Chris and around the desk toward Sydney, who stood up and gestured for the door.

"Caleb, you need to leave. You know I have a restraining order, and you are not allowed on school property. I'm asking you nicely to go, but if you don't I will call the police." He grabbed her arm that was directing him toward the door and pulled her up against his body, jerking her forward violently. At that, Chris rose and cleared his throat calmly.

It drew the man's attention and he shouted at Chris, "Get the hell out of here, this has nothing to do with you."

"Actually, I was in the middle of a meeting. So why don't you go? It sounds like, of the two of us, I'm the one without a legal obligation to leave." Chris didn't make a move for the man, he did nothing but stand his ground confidently. Over the years he'd learned that a calm expression in the face of danger made more impact than an angry one.

The man reached into his coat pocket, pulled out a kitchen knife and waved it in Chris's direction. Sydney let out a shrill yelp, and he jerked her forward again. "How about I cut off your damn head and mail it to your mother? Get the hell out of here."

Chris smirked wryly at the man. Sydney's eyes were wild and wet with tears, but as she caught a glimpse of Chris's rebellious indifference to the danger, she quieted her whimpering. Maybe he knew something she didn't.

"First of all, you couldn't cut someone's head off with that blade. It's dull and much too short. It would take a whole day to get through the spinal cord. You don't have that kind of time. Second, my mother, God rest her soul," Chris said, making the sign of the cross as he spoke, "died five years ago alongside my father. She wouldn't be there to receive the package. Not to mention the US Postal Service has numerous check points to ensure body parts and other illegal items aren't shipped. I learned that the hard way." He paused and shook his head at the memory.

"And finally, the likelihood that you'd even have the stomach to handle a severed head long enough to package it in bubble wrap is slim. Long story short, your plan doesn't seem very plausible. Do you have another idea? Perhaps we can brainstorm a bit." Chris had been in countless scenarios like this before. He had earned a notorious reputation for being a smart ass when everyone else was shitting their pants in fear.

"I could just stab you," the man shouted, jabbing the knife closer to Chris, "and then I'll kill her. This bitch deserves it for what she did to me." He pointed the knife back toward Sydney, and Chris knew the situation was reaching a climax. He had hoped campus security would be on scene but he heard no sign of them.

"I was hoping you weren't going to say that." Chris reached down slowly and pulled his concealed Walther P99 pistol from the holster on his ankle. He knew the kid with the knife was not a professional. He'd probably never stared down a gun before, and he certainly wasn't expecting Chris to be carrying one. "If you stab me, I'm going to shoot you. Do you know how many men I've shot in my life? Quite a few. How many people have you stabbed with your steak knife? You seem like a smart kid," Chris said, furrowing his brows and raising his arm to point the gun at the man's head. "Why don't you let her go? Otherwise, there'll be a cleaning crew in here tonight scraping your brain matter off the walls."

The man shifted Sydney in front of himself and put the blade up to her neck. She fought back the urge to scream as cold steel pressed into her skin. Her eyes met Chris's and he could see her fighting to stay composed.

"I don't really mind shooting her," Chris said offhandedly. "I'm pretty sure she was about to fire me. So if you want to use her as a human shield and think that's going to stop me, you have me confused with some do-gooder cop. I'm not a cop. I'm the opposite of a cop. I'm the guy who shoots you right in the face, just to see your teeth fly out of your mouth. I'm the guy that gets off watching you gasp for your last breath, knowing I'm the one who took it from you. You with your steak knife, you're not that guy. So, because I'd like to make it home for dinner tonight instead of dealing with all the bullshit that will come from killing you, this is your last chance. Let her go, put the knife down, and go sit in that chair until the cops come to haul your ass away. Or you can die. Take a good look around this room. Is this the last place you want to see before I kill you?" Chris could see beads of sweat gathering on the man's forehead. His hand was shaking now, his knuckles were white where they gripped the black handle of his knife. He loosened his hold on Sydney and shoved her down into her office chair. He backed up slowly, dropping the knife onto the floor and moving to the chair in the corner of the room. He was crying now, sobbing incoherent apologies.

Sydney didn't move, she locked eyes with Chris and sat completely still. He had expected her to be shaking, wailing, maybe even run into his arms. Instead she seemed almost as frightened of him as she had been of the man with the knife.

"Put the gun down," a man shouted as he entered the room. Chris lowered his gun to the floor and raised his arms over his head. The officer approached him and secured the gun then proceeded to forcefully cuff him.

"Wait," cried Sydney, "he didn't do anything wrong. He saved my life. That man, Caleb, he came in here with a knife and threatened to kill me. Chris stopped him." It was the first time Sydney had called him by anything other than Mr. King, and he loved how his name sounded on her lips. The officer told Chris to take a seat but didn't make a move to remove the handcuffs. It didn't matter though. He'd perfected sitting comfortably while restrained. It was a regular event in his old life.

Two more officers entered the room, and there was an enormous amount of commotion and chatter as Sydney frantically tried to explain the situation. She grew more and more upset as the officers began to read Chris his rights. "What has he done? He saved my life, you can't arrest him."

The oldest of the officers in the room approached Sydney, trying to calm her. "Ma'am I completely understand how upsetting this is, and the courage Mr. King showed here today is admirable. But firearms are banned from campus. Illinois does not allow concealed carry, and on top of that he does not have a Firearm's Owner Identification Card. He's violated a significant number of laws here today by carrying that weapon. We don't have a choice but to arrest him. I've got a supervisor en route now. He'll hopefully be able to advise us on the best way to handle this very unique situation. In the meantime, Officer Krito will stay here with both of you while my partner and I book Caleb. I'm very sorry, Mr. King, and I do hope this works out well for you. I believe you saved lives today." The man tipped his head apologetically at both of them as he led Caleb, still sobbing, out of the room.

Sydney sat down next to Chris and put her hand on his leg, immediately realizing that was far too intimate. It was too late though, pulling it away suddenly would look far more inappropriate than letting it linger there. "I am so sorry. Caleb is my ex-boyfriend. I've been dealing with him for so long, but I never thought it would come to this. I promise I'll do everything I can to keep you from getting in trouble. My uncle is a skip tracer. He works with these guys all the time. Maybe he can pull some strings." Sydney was talking so quickly that she wasn't catching enough breath to keep her from getting lightheaded.

"Sydney, calm down," Chris said, wishing his hands were free and he could caress her soft, tear-stained cheek. "I need you to do me two favors. In my pants pocket there is a business card, can you reach in and get it for me?" He leaned himself over and she stared at him skeptically.

An hour ago he was asking if she had plastic surgery, forty minutes ago he was saving her life, now he wanted her to go fishing around his pants pocket. This was the oddest progression of a work relationship that she had ever experienced. Finally, she reached her hand in and felt the rock hard muscle of his thigh. She hesitantly moved her fingers, exploring his pocket, desperately trying not to touch anything that might make her blush. When she felt the sharp edge of the business card, she sighed with relief and pulled it out.

"I need you to call that number and speak with Jason. Tell him who you are and everything that happened here today. Tell him we're in the red, and that he needs to come here now. If he doesn't get here before they take me to the police station then he'll have to meet me there. That's where the second favor comes in. My son, Little Chris, will be getting off the bus at

197

three-fifteen. I need you to meet him, let him into the house and stay with him until I get home. In my wallet you'll find my address, and a picture of my son. When you see him say "Cherry Coke," then he'll know it's safe to go with you. He'll know how to set all the alarms when you get in the house. With any luck I'll be out by dinner time and this will all be over."

"All of this is a little overwhelming," Sydney trembled. "Who are you? All those things you said to Caleb, you don't sound like a normal person." She leaned back again, slightly frightened of who she might be dealing with.

"It's a very long story. I don't have anyone I can trust with my son. He's my whole world, Sydney. I need to know you'll take care of him until Jason can get the rest of this squared away." Chris could understand her hesitation. She clearly hadn't had much luck with men, and he'd certainly laid it on thick while trying to get Caleb to lower his gun.

"Of course," Sydney gulped, knowing she owed Chris her life. The least she could do was care for his son while he dealt with the legal ramifications of intervening. "Where's your wallet?" she asked, ready to follow his instructions.

Chris had a mischievous smile and winked at her as he spoke, "It's in the other pocket."

Can't wait to read the next book in the Piper Anderson Series?

Go to AuthorDanielleStewart.com and add your email address to the mailing list.

We'll send you an email as soon as
Changing Fate
is released

Proof